THE BITTER DAYS OF
FINIS McCANLESS

Also by James Wyckoff

LARS
JOHN SLAUGHTER'S WAY
SLATER'S BOOK
SHARKEY

THE BITTER DAYS OF FINIS McCANLESS

JAMES WYCKOFF

DOUBLEDAY & COMPANY, INC.
GARDEN CITY, NEW YORK
1981

All of the characters in this book are fictitious, and any resemblance to actual persons, living or dead, is purely coincidental.

Library of Congress Cataloging in Publication Data

Wyckoff, James.
  The bitter days of Finis McCanless.

  I. Title.
      PS3573.Y3B5   813'.54
      ISBN: 0-385-15830-0
            AACR2
Library of Congress Catalog Card Number 80-2633
Copyright © 1981 by James Wyckoff
First Edition
All Rights Reserved
Printed in the United States of America

THE BITTER DAYS OF
FINIS McCANLESS

CHAPTER 1

Seen from across the valley, the horse and rider appeared indistinguishable from the few trees and rocks that met the high blue sky. Only in movement as they now broke out of the horizon did they become clear to the watching men in the little box canyon.

The rider did not see the watchers. They were protected by a stand of cottonwoods. But he did catch the sudden flight of the jay flashing out of the trees and his eyes sharpened.

Shifting in the battered stock saddle, he eased the holstered .45 at his right hip. He was not expecting trouble— no more than a man might figure on as routine when riding through new country—for no one was expecting him; of that he was sure.

Even so, he was keened to all possibilities, as was customary with him; not altering the slow, almost picking gait of the little dun gelding. It had been a long ride and he had pushed himself and the pony, both of them now dusty from the trails through the red-colored country. He was tired, but only he knew that; it did not show.

Seen close now, he was a lean, muscular man of medium height, in his thirties, with widely spaced blue eyes at the corners of which could be seen the faint imprint of crow's-feet. Clearly, he was a man of the trail, a man who lived by the weather, the land, and by swift calculation and action in the face of danger. And as some told it back in the Sweetwater country, a man with a humor tough as whang leather. No man to get previous with, they told it back on the Sweetwater. McCanless. The name taken from a package of plug tobacco left at the site of a fired wagon train.

All that hot forenoon he and the dun had followed the thin, hard trail west and north toward the Big Horns. Now with the sun straight up he could feel that heat in the brim of his dusty brown Stetson hat as he lifted and resettled it, breaking the band of sweat that encircled his head.

As he rode, his light, almost sky-blue eyes took in the detail of the dry land, and he figured how much stock could graze there, for how long. He thought too how the whole of the Wyoming country was already overgrazed and overstocked and more than likely soon would be picked bone clean.

A long journey for sure. And he was still not easy with the likes of Big Jaw Henrique and Whiskey Bill Cuttles, the two he had left back at Cohoes riding herd on the town; the one an old buzzard who'd talk any man to his knees, the other generally so ornery and drunk that they told it he'd been shot in the head a dozen years ago and was afraid to sober up for fear of dropping dead from the bullet. But they were all he could get on such short notice. And besides, they had sided him—McCanless, marshal of Cohoes on the Sweetwater, a town just pulling itself out from the cattle wars which had swept the land like a tornado of blood, then moved on to the Big Horn country.

But Wiley Hinges had written a letter and so McCanless found himself riding to a place he'd never heard of, a place named Horsehead. He was not sorry quitting the lawman's job. He had never figured himself a lawman.

He shifted again in the saddle, his eyes flicking to the

stand of cottonwoods, but there was no sign. Nothing. Still, he had that familiar, funny feeling. Yes, by God, he was tuckered. But he knew how to keep awake. Wiley had taught him how to keep awake. And a lot of things.

Yes—Wiley. Funny, him ending up a cattleman after all those years of owlhooting. But better than dancing on the end of a posse rope, better than topping off broncs for board and found and ending up with your guts all busted.

More than a few times Wiley'd spoken of one day catching himself a spread and running his own brand. And by God he'd gone and done it. He himself though— hell, he was still packing a gun, still looking to the far horizon. Maybe when he got to be Wiley's age—Wiley had always told him, "Boy, you got a lot to learn"—maybe he'd settle something by then.

Ten years it had been—no, more like eight—since Wiley'd pulled up stakes and ridden out, telling him he was a man now and he'd by God taught him all there was and now it was up to himself to use it one way or the other. Left him with his learning and his old Deane & Adams, now in his warbag tied back of the cantle on the stock saddle. McCanless' sole heirloom.

A bead of sweat had just rolled onto his eyelid and he had blinked and raised his arm to wipe it away with his shirtsleeve when, in that divided second, he caught the glint of sunlight on metal and everything he was came to that quickness he had always known. Digging heels to the spooked dun, he ducked low over the saddle horn as the bullet whined across his back and off into the wide blue sky.

Something slammed his shoulder and he was on the ground rolling, his right hand striking for the .45. Almost before he stopped in a clump of sage the three men were upon him.

"Moved kinda fast for to of missed you with the Winchester." The big, black-bearded face stank of whiskey and tobacco. "Where you figure you be headin'?"

From somewhere in his sawing throat McCanless collected enough spittle to splatter it into that leering face. As he did so, he slumped, twisted, let his body go limp. The three were caught off guard, and now he swiftly drove down with his heel on the bearded man's instep and kneed him in the groin. Twisting, he smashed one of the others in the pit of the stomach and as he doubled hit him again in the neck.

But they were on him. And they were big and fast. Yet, he was holding his own until suddenly his legs gave way. The bearded one had hit him in the back of the knees with a singletree. He lay on his back on the ground with the Winchester pointed right between his eyes.

"I asta question!" The big man with the black beard stood over him, his words driving down over his big belly, which was heaving from his exertions.

"Bisbee, whyn't you just pull the trigger and be shut of the sonofabitch," said one of his companions, a man with a very long, drooping mustache and large, drooping trousers.

Bisbee spat. "Kenny, you are a knothead! You know the orders."

"Course I know the orders."

"Then why'n hell you throwed down on him when you knowed we're only s'posed to warn them off!"

"I was just tryin' to wing him," Kenny replied imperturbably. "But now looky here, he has hurt *us*. Hit me in the mouth, clobbered Gorm, and he knocked you right on yer royal ass. Knocked off Gorm's hat he did." And Kenny's long face broke into a malicious grin, while Bisbee and the man named Gorm scowled furiously.

Gorm was a thin, knobby man. "Why don't we give him the treatment," he said softly. "He is askin' for it.

And *them* was our orders for any tough ones, for sure."
He was dusting his gray derby hat with the sleeve of his
shirt. Now, holding the derby carefully with the brim between his fingers, he placed it carefully on top of his little
head.

"He is tough all right," Bisbee agreed as he poked the
barrel of the Winchester into McCanless' neck. "Get up,"
he said. "But real slow. I personally will gut shoot you if
you try any more funny moves."

Standing at last, he felt the pain in his wounded shoulder. He knew it was bleeding, but judged it to be a flesh
wound; no broken bone. Still, he gave only a moment's attention to this; there was the action at hand. He stood
very still, letting his body relax in order to collect all the
strength he could.

"What you doin' here in this here country?" Gorm demanded.

"Riding through. What does it look like."

Bisbee said, "Not through this country you ain't."

"It is unfenced range, mister."

"Not to you it ain't."

Gorm said, "Give him the treatment. He looks like a
mavericker to me. It'll remind him, and he can tell his
buddies."

"Where'd you think you was riding to, huh?" It was
Kenny who spoke, the one with the drooping mustache.

"Montana."

"That's a long ride."

"It wasn't so long till you damn fools stopped me."

"Say, Kenny, you reckon he might be a lawman—huh?"
It was Gorm, touching the brim of his derby hat.

Suddenly Bisbee jammed the barrel of the Winchester
in his stomach. "You a lawman?"

"If I was, do you think I'd say so, you damn fool!"

"We got ways of makin' you talk."

"He is still sassy," Gorm said, smooth. "I am sayin' we ought to . . ."

"All right then," Bisbee cut in. "He has asked for it." He stepped back, but with the Winchester still holding the prisoner. Suddenly he spat. "You and Kenny tend to it," he said. Then he spat again, his eyes squinting at McCanless. "Mebbe the law is after you, eh?"

"That's the size of it."

"I say he is a gun for the maverickers," Gorm said, suddenly appearing from behind him, the singletree in his hand. "You working for Hinges?"

"Never heard of him." McCanless said it slow and even. By God, he was thinking, by God it looked like he'd ridden right into another range war.

Gorm stepped real close, still holding the singletree. "I says you are a hired gun for Hinges and them goddam maverickers."

"Get the fire goin'," Bisbee ordered. "Don't matter who he is, he won't be back here in a hurry." Reaching up with his left hand, he scratched deep into his thick beard along his neck; his other hand never moved on the Winchester, with the forefinger curled close on the trigger.

Behind him he heard the first crackle of burning wood, like little pistol shots, and the air was suddenly heavy with the smell of pitch.

"Put your hands back of you," Bisbee snapped.

He moved his arms slowly, for the shoulder was hurting. But someone behind him was impatient and grabbed his wrists and began lashing them together.

Bisbee said, "How is she doin'?"

"Hot enough." Kenny appeared from behind him with a running iron in his hand.

"Give it a touch more." Gorm's voice was as flat as a board.

Bisbee took a step toward McCanless, but still carefully, even though the prisoner had little chance with his hands tied behind his back and a rifle pointed at his chest.

Now Bisbee's corded breath drove his words as he spoke, the stench of old tobacco and rotten teeth reaching McCanless like a blow.

"You maverickers like to use that running iron, so we figure you might like to have a little used on yourself. It's the warning. When we don't kill you we give you the warning. Next time—if there is a next time—it will be slow bullets. And maybe the iron, too," he added. He waited a moment, his little eyes gleaming. "You stay off of this here land. This be Broken Spade range, and don't you never forget it."

McCanless looked straight at the big man, forcing himself to keep from again spitting into that leering face.

"How come you are so all-fired scared of strangers?" he said.

Bisbee's forehead wrinkled as he opened his eyes wide and stared at the prisoner. "You are just ridin' through, mister. Remember that. Just do not forget that." And his big face closed again. "You'll stay off Broken Spade land from this day," he said.

"Or he'll stay in it," Gorm said, reappearing. "Like permanent." He was smoking a cigar and holding the running iron, which was white hot. And all at once McCanless remembered the raid—way back it had been— on the Adams express car with Wiley and the boys, and Cupid Tebeau firing the car after shooting the guard. Wiley'd been real graveled at that.

Still holding the Winchester in one hand, Bisbee took the iron with the other. He spat suddenly on the white heat, the spittle sizzling swiftly into smoke.

A blow in the back of McCanless' legs knocked him to his knees, and Gorm and Kenny had him on his back; one with a knee across his throat, the other sitting on his legs.

Bisbee looked down into his face, then he reached down and ripped open his shirt.

He tried to let himself go loose, the better to handle the pain that would come. But the play was to be more refined than he had thought. He felt the heat of the iron coming closer to his chest; waited for the metal to hit him. But Bisbee held it just away, not touching him with the iron, letting the heat work by itself.

"If there's a next time," he heard Gorm's voice saying, "it'll be all the way. Figger yerself lucky."

The iron was removed. The men stood up. While they watched, McCanless got slowly to his feet, his hands still tied behind his back. Gorm was smoking his cigar and now and again touching the brim of his derby hat with his fingertips as though to make sure it was still there. Now Kenny stepped forward, a barlow knife in his hand, and McCanless' bonds were cut.

"Git on an' git out," Bisbee said, pointing the Winchester toward the ground-hitched dun.

McCanless stood dazed, his chest tearing at him, his left arm hanging limp at his side.

Yet it was the pain that helped him, focusing his anger and clearing his head. He tried moving his wounded arm. And he remembered Wiley telling him never to take a situation on another man's terms, but to use everything for himself. "Use what's at hand," Wiley had so often told him. "If you bin shot or hurt, figure a way to make use of it."

He knew exactly what he was going to do. With the wound in his shoulder and the burn on his chest, he would be expected to stagger to his horse and ride off. They had taken his .45 and the Winchester he carried in the boot alongside his saddle. Clearly, he had only one option. By some miracle no one had checked his warbag tied to the saddle skirt. He was visualizing exactly how he would open the bag and get his hand on Wiley's Deane & Adams.

The three were watching him carefully, their hands near their weapons, while he walked very slowly toward the dun pony. Twice he staggered, nearly falling, pretending a dizziness and pain much greater than he really felt.

Very slowly he checked the dun, his saddle rigging and bridle.

"Hustle it," Gorm snapped.

McCanless took his time, checking his warbag to see that it was secure, risking that it might suddenly occur to them to take a look, but actually loosening the bag and one of the leather strings that secured it.

Finally, he gathered the reins and a handful of the animal's mane in his left hand and stepped carefully into the stirrup, swinging his right leg over the cantle. He sat in the saddle a moment, as though collecting himself, then checked his lariat rope, reaching, to his side away from the men, the opening to the warbag.

"I could use my armaments," he said, kneeing the horse closer to the three men.

At this they all burst out laughing.

"That is a funny," Kenny said. "On account of we can use 'em ourselves."

"Now git," Bisbee said, real sharp.

But McCanless had used the moment to spook the dun; now evidently having difficulty with him. He kept kicking the animal on the side away from the men, yanking at his mouth at the same time with the reins and bit.

"He rides that animal like it was a locomotive," Gorm said real sour.

And as he spoke, with the dun prancing some, McCanless reached behind him and pulled at the strips of whang leather that held the bag to the saddle. These he had tied originally in his usual way, with a horse knot so that one quick pull freed it.

"What the hell you doin'?" snarled Bisbee.

"Just looking for some medicine," McCanless said, and he pulled a bottle of whiskey out of the warbag.

"Well—looky here!" cried Gorm. And McCanless, on the high-stepping pony, watched the three faces light up eagerly.

"We will take care of that toothache healer," Kenny said, and moved toward the man on the horse.

McCanless swiftly raised the bottle to his lips and took a good swallow, yet always with his eyes on the others. God, it was good. It was really good, as it raced all the way down through his body.

Bringing the bottle down with a gasp of pleasure, he turned sideways in the saddle, purposely not recorking the bottle, maneuvering the animal so that it was almost alongside the three men.

"Give that over," Kenny said.

"Here." And McCanless tossed the uncorked bottle to Bisbee, to his left hand, which was holding the Winchester. At the same instant, he kicked the dun pony and jerked his head back and up so that he reared, his hooves pawing over the surprised men, a wild whinny breaking from him. The three men were totally caught in their surprise and greed as the horse reared and the open bottle of whiskey came flying through the air.

McCanless was out of the saddle with the warbag, one hand still holding the reins to keep the horse close as protection while his other hand streaked to the Deane & Adams. Landing on his feet, he fell to his knees, but was up in an instant. At no time was he not in charge, while the dun's hooves flailed the air and the three men rushed out of the way.

"Goddammit!" Bisbee screamed as a hoof brushed him, knocking him sideways.

Cool as a whisper McCanless raised Wiley's Deane & Adams and shot Bisbee through the neck.

Kenny meanwhile had drawn his own handgun and had pumped two shots at McCanless, who, without moving his feet, shot him in the chest.

Gorm, swiftly sizing the situation, sprang onto a little pinto and took off down the trail. McCanless had a momentary impulse to follow, but the dun had been nicked in the withers and was badly spooked; while he himself was suddenly feeling weak. He pumped two shots after Gorm, one close enough for the fleeing horseman to grab at his derby hat.

McCanless stood watching him out of sight, his legs spread for support, still holding his horse by the reins, still holding the six-gun. Both Bisbee and Kenny were dead and there was nothing to do now except pick up the half empty bottle of whiskey, which had landed in a clump of sagebrush, and have a drink. Which he did. And he savored it all the way through his battered body.

He tore a piece off his bandanna and corked the bottle, retrieved his .45 and rifle; then checked the dun's rig and mounted.

He was hurting now. His shoulder was bleeding, so he bandaged it as best he could with the bandanna. But it was his chest that really hurt. It burned like fire. Only once before in his life had Finis McCanless felt fire. That had been when he was eight years old. When he had met Wiley Hinges.

CHAPTER 2

"It is him."

Gorm's sharp little eyes had picked out the horse and rider the moment they came off the trail just beyond the cattle pens and depot.

"Who?"

"Him who shot up Bisbee and Kenny."

Gorm and his companion were standing just inside the front parlor window at Long Nose Alice's place. This establishment stood at the outskirts of Horsehead, in that section of town known as Fever Park.

Gorm, expressionless beneath his eternal derby hat—now with a neat bullet hole in front and back—stood rigid as a corral pole, his knobby jaws chewing vigorously on a plug of tobacco.

His words were spoken to a short, wiry man in tight-fitting shirt and pants, and a white, wide-brimmed Stetson hat. This was Harry Dime, foreman of the Broken Spade. A dour man, at the moment sucking on a wooden lucifer, switching it from one side of his mouth to the other, but slowly, ruminatively.

Harry Dime's face was shiny, with an orange tint to it, as though he'd had too much sunlight. He moved closer to the window, but not crowding Gorm. Harry Dime was a neat man, even a bit fastidious, and since Gorm fidgeted a good deal and took up a lot of space, the foreman kept his distance. Gorm had always irritated him; he wasn't sure whether he disliked more his rigidity or his fidgeting.

But Gorm was handy with a gun, and since Cole O'Bannion had brought in regulators for his range, he was of use. But the foreman was especially irritated with Gorm at the moment, not only because of the fiasco out at the box canyon, but also for his being here at Alice's at just the time of his own visit. Harry Dime didn't mind now and again drinking with his men, but that was where he drew the line.

"No," he said, suddenly putting his hand hard on Gorm's arm as it moved toward his holstered six-gun. "Not now. Not here."

Gorm, drawing away abruptly, said, "Aw shit!"

"Don't let him see you," Harry Dime said, driven by his annoyance to pull further authority on Gorm.

"He don't look too bad," Gorm said, sniffing and rubbing his belly.

Harry Dime moved the wooden match across his mouth. "Where you figger he has been this past day or two?"

"Maybe resting," Gorm answered laconically, and a corner of his mouth twitched as he felt the wry humor of his remark.

"The hell."

As he studied the situation, Gorm's chewing speeded up, his jaws going fast as a prairie dog's. Then he suddenly let fly a streak of brown and yellow saliva at a nearby cuspidor, his aim not wholly accurate.

"Told us he was headin' for Montana country."

"Mebbe he is."

"He is a lyin' sonofabitch," Gorm said. "By God, a man cannot trust a one. Not a one these days."

"He a lawman you figger?" Harry Dime took the lucifer out of his mouth and began scratching inside his ear with it, both men keeping their eyes on the horse and rider.

"If he be one, he is as good as a dead one." Gorm again appreciated his own sense of humor and let his tight face spread in a slow grin, while he scratched deep, first under one armpit and then the other.

"Keep back from the winder," Harry Dime warned, stern, again speaking from his irritation.

"Said he was just ridin' through," Gorm said, unable to leave it alone; and he began sucking his gums.

Harry Dime scowled but said nothing.

The horse and rider were level with the window now.

Gorm sniffed. "Be a funny if he was headed for right here." And he coughed out a sort of laugh. When his foreman offered no response, he felt suddenly uneasy and said, "O'Bannion ain't goin' to favor this."

The foreman turned swiftly on him. "I don't like it, Gorm. I don't like it!" Harry Dime's face had turned a deeper hue. "I do not like what happened out there when the three of you braced him, and I for sure do not favor that sonofabitch ridin' into town here. Who in hell is he, is what I want to know!"

A startled look fell across Gorm's face, but then he collected himself and his eyes became even smaller as they turned from the window to Harry Dime. "I am drawing my pay from Cole O'Bannion . . ."

But Harry Dime braced him before he could say more. "You are working for me, and don't you never forget that!" And even though he was shorter than Gorm, he stood hard right there in front of him, his clothes tight as paint on his solid, muscular body. "I hired you," he went on, "and Bisbee and Kenny, and by God you remember that!"

It was a moment; and it was Gorm who backed down, turning to the window again.

"We will corral it," Harry Dime said. Seeing he had won, his tone was easier. "He is trouble for sure." And he shoved his hands into his tooled leather belt and pointed with his chin to the retreating back of the rider.

"What'll we do about him?" Gorm said.

"We will kill him," Harry Dime said. "But when me or Mister O'Bannion says so."

They were both silent as they watched the horse and rider moving closer into the town.

CHAPTER 3

McCanless rode slowly past the cattle pens, the railroad depot, past the house of Long Nose Alice and the shanties that made up Fever Park. He rode carefully to accommodate the pain that was still in his body even after a day and night, which he had spent at a deserted line-camp he'd found when he was just about done in and near falling out of the saddle.

It was a one-room cabin, and he'd managed enough strength to picket the dun and get inside before passing out. When he later came to, he did what he could to dress his shoulder, but there wasn't anything he could do about his chest, save drink the whiskey. But there was grub in the cabin, as well as firewood. He decided not to force a ride to Horsehead, but to rest. Besides, for all he knew he might run into more trouble, and he was not ready for that. So he remained that night and the next day, taking the trail the following night. He discovered then that in his pain and fatigue he had been going in the wrong direction. It was afternoon when he finally reached Horsehead.

He rode with care now, seeing everything, yet without moving his head much. Like any man seasoned to the trail or danger, he knew that you could see a lot more if you didn't stare directly, if you didn't get caught in what you were looking at. Wiley had taught him that when he was still a button.

He had indeed spotted someone watching from the unpainted house at the edge of town, but he did not know who it was, maybe somebody simply sizing the weather. But he could see right off that Horsehead was a lively place. Just as old Whiskey Bill Cuttles had told him when he'd said where he was heading, a town where most of the doors swung both ways, a town with the hair on.

The hitchracks were crowded, so he decided on the livery stable, but then he saw a place just outside the Golden Wedding Saloon, which stood between Sayles' General Store and the Bronco Eatery.

Dismounting was painful but he managed without showing his condition to any of the hangers-on outside the Golden Wedding. He had spotted the shingle hanging above the small doorway next to the General Store. "C. McGee—Doctor of Medicine," it said. But there was another sign on the door itself, handwritten, stating that the doctor was away on a call and would be back "soon."

Without a break in his stride, McCanless moved past the doorway and entered Sayles' General Store.

A heavyset man wearing yellow galluses and a wide leather belt greeted him.

"I am needing some ammo," McCanless said, approaching the worn wooden counter.

The storekeeper's eyes flicked to the holstered .45. "For the Colt?" His air was friendly, his black hair was combed close to his head; his hands were puffy, and McCanless noted as he pushed his wares forward on the counter that there was no indentation between the knuckles.

"Two boxes will do 'er for now," McCanless said, "and two for the Winchester," he added, ".44-.40."

"First time in this part of the country?" the storekeeper asked pleasantly. He was an expansive man; his body was big, but his skin seemed even bigger, hanging on his large frame like a loose sack.

The storekeeper flushed a little as his customer accepted the ammunition and paid out money without answering his question.

"Quiet in town," he resumed, trying to pick it up again. "Course it'll be a whole lot livelier come the Fourth. Horsehead always goes it big on the Fourth of July, and this year'll be bigger than ever. Going to have a tightrope walker and a prizefight championship."

"I am looking for a man name of Wiley Hinges," McCanless said, looking directly at the other man. "Know him, do you?"

The words seemed to be put both as question and flat statement, and the storekeeper wasn't ready for that.

"Suggest you ask down to the marshal's office," he replied carefully. Then he licked his lips, his eyes darting over some tables of merchandise while he hitched at his big leather belt.

McCanless picked up the boxes of cartridges and turned to go.

As he put his hand on the doorknob the storekeeper said, "I'm Clem Sayles. I'm a councilman here in Horsehead; and this here is my store." He let a little laugh pop out of his suddenly tense face. "Just want you to know you are welcome."

"Good enough." McCanless gave a nod as he opened the door and stepped outside.

Clem Sayles stood in the open doorway. "I didn't catch your name, mister."

McCanless looked directly at him. There had been something strange in the way the storekeeper had responded to his question about Wiley. "That's right," he said. "You didn't."

The marshal's office was only a few yards down the street, but the door was locked, and he could see no sign of life as he peered through the grimy window glass. A lounger was seated on the stoop outside, chewing something or other—maybe tobacco—and breathing rotgut into the clean prairie air. McCanless was feeling the pain in his chest and shoulder enough that he was in no mood for the local's thrust of laconic humor when he asked the marshal's whereabouts.

"Marshal's up to the cemetery, stranger."

"Funeral, huh."

"Reckon." The lounger wore a battered Stetson hat with a ragged hole in the crown and he looked like a busted-up bronc topper from an earlier day; too old and too beat-up to ride any green stuff, and more than likely too ornery to do much else than drink and run his mouth. He spat indolently now at a pile of fresh horse manure in the street and watched McCanless with a glint in his eye.

Something about that look and the way he had spoken caught McCanless, and he stepped off the boardwalk into the street and looked down at the old bronc rider.

"Mister, I asked you a straight question and I am figurin' on gettin' a straight answer and not some of that goddam local humor."

The humor in the other's face and eyes faded right now; his adam's apple pumped a couple of times as he suddenly came to. But his courage was gone only for a moment. He eased back into himself as he said, "They are plantin' the marshal. How come he is at the cemetery." And he nodded his head a few times as though agreeing with himself.

"I am looking for a man name of Wiley Hinges," McCanless said.

The man on the stoop looked at him now plumb center. "Mister, I done just told you where he is. Marshal Hinges, by now he'll be in heaven, or hell—one."

CHAPTER 4

The Thermopolis House had been moved to Horsehead from Crow River two years before, when the railroad extended its spur to create a new cattle terminal. It was the building, McCanless shortly discovered, of which the citizens were most proud—for its big crystal chandelier in the high-ceilinged lobby, its big mahogany desk, its gold-framed mirrors, potted plants, thick rugs, fine furniture, and ornate brass cuspidors. All of this spoke of the wealth which—if not presently bulging the coffers of the town and the pockets of the local merchants—was fully expected, since the biggest season in cattle history was predicted.

But that was on the ground floor. In the little room one flight up it was hot. McCanless had drawn the shade on the one window to thwart the sunlight streaming through, but it didn't help all that much. So he'd stripped and now lay flat on his back on the bed. Not to sleep. He could have used sleep, a lot of it, and indeed he still felt a good deal of pain in his shoulder and especially in his chest. Only he did not lie down in order to sleep, but to figure his strategy, to put together the pieces of all that had happened and see what to do.

He had arrived at the cemetery while the funeral was in progress. There were not many people there. The preacher read the standard burial service quickly, and then the gravediggers lifted their shovels. He was just as

glad for the brevity, not being one for drawn-out fare-
wells.

At graveside he had studied the mourners. Standing
apart from the rest were three older men, clearly cow
waddies and very likely fellow cardplayers too. Then
there was a small group of sober-faced gents who proved
to be members of the town council, joined he noticed by
Clem Sayles, who avoided his eyes. Standing next to a
pretty young girl was a short, barrel-shaped man with a
head of thick gray hair, a broomlike mustache, also gray,
and sideburns, slightly darker. Peering out from all that
hair was a ruddy face. Doctor McGee, he found out later.
He wondered who the girl was. Clearly, she was not one
of the assorted curiosity seekers. Wiley, of course, had no
relatives—only, in a manner of speaking, himself, whom
the mourners looked at questioningly.

But he was in for yet another surprise, for from the
very mouth of the preacher he learned that Wiley had
been married and that in fact he was being buried "beside his beloved wife, Lillian, who died of the pneumonia
just a year ago."

Wiley had not died of the pneumonia, however. Wiley
Hinges, marshal of Horsehead, had been shot in the back.
He had been murdered.

McCanless lay on the bed in the heated room turning it
all over. He had read the letter more than a few times. It
was all Wiley, for sure. Short. To the point.

"Hello Fin—Have bin running some 250 head on fair
range. And no Texas fever, and working with stove up
cowhands who be more trouble than help, I bin cuttin it
alright. Some good games of stud, in which I won this
spread. And some not so good. There is a sonofabitch
here Cole O'Bannion thinks he owns it all. The way the
boys tell it God changed his name to O'Bannion about a
dozen years back. I am sending my deed to the outfit and

brand as I expect some trouble. How are you. Your good friend Wiley Hinges."

The same Wiley. Trouble. But nothing in the letter about taking the marshal's job, or getting married. And not asking for help. Except he was asking, wasn't he? Anyhow, McCanless had come. But God, Wiley a lawman? Wiley Hinges, who'd ridden with Kid Bollinger, Ace Cummings, Tebeau, and God knows who else!

Then Doc McGee had filled in a lot of it for him. McCanless had found him in his office directly after the funeral. Up close, Doc seemed even shorter, even more like a barrel, for he was clearly solid, even though his jowls quivered like turkey wattles whenever he got excited, which was frequent.

"McGee. Corliss McGee. Call me Doc or McGee. Not Corliss," he said, his eyes wide on his visitor. The eyes were basically hazel-colored, but laced with a multitude of red lines.

"McCanless."

"Shoulder, eh."

McCanless nodded, quick to appreciate the doc's keenness of observation.

"Noticed it at the funeral," McGee said.

"And my chest." McCanless was removing his shirt.

Doc McGee fell silent, except for a very low whistling between his teeth, almost a breathing, while he stood contemplating his patient.

"McCanless." Doc repeated the name ruminatively as he removed from his shirt pocket a pair of gold-rimmed spectacles and wiped them carefully with a red bandanna taken from his hip. "McCanless." Like he was tasting the word.

"Don't get around too much any longer," he went on, in an allowing tone of voice. "Can't see too good, can't ride a helluva lot with the damn rheumatiz, and I am carrying lead from being shot up in one of them battles in the war. Can't recollect which one since they was all alike. The battles not the wars, I mean . . ." And he rambled on, coughing, wheezing, and now and again belching softly. "Everybody hollerin' and runnin' about cussin' and scared and all that, and more often than not shootin' one another 'stead of the enemy. Which happened to me. Got shot up by my own side."

The flow stopped momentarily as he bent toward his patient. His hands were quick, gentle, sure. They knew what they were doing.

"Hmm." Examining the shoulder. "Likely a .44–.40, I would allow." And then the chest. "So you run into O'Bannion's regulators. I have heard of their handiwork." He sat down in his chair, his thick, short hands resting on his thick thighs.

"Who is O'Bannion?" McCanless asked, reaching for his shirt.

"No, I got to dress those," Doc said.

"I was lookin' for my makings."

"Go ahead." He sniffed. "O'Bannion? He is the Broken Spade and he is the big man in this country. Or, now I should say he was."

"And Wiley crossed him."

"Wiley crossed him with his Circle Double O."

"You're saying O'Bannion wanted that range."

McGee nodded. Suddenly he stood up, though he had to take a quick step to keep his balance. "Damn rheumatiz," he muttered as he crossed to a large cabinet on the other side of the room. "I'll be giving you a herb for that burn. Got it from a Arapaho medicine man." He bent down, still speaking with his back to his patient. "It should help. You look to me like you bin around this good while so you'll maybe know this will help." He turned, squinting at McCanless. "Course, on the other hand, maybe not." He barked out a cough. "No, you are a good bit like Wiley Hinges, I can tell." He advanced toward McCanless, carrying the medicine.

For several moments he addressed himself completely to his patient's wounds, working in silence, wheezing, just humming to himself very softly now and again; doing a neat, professional job, McCanless could see.

"Good thing you didn't get blood poisoning from either one," Doc said finally, straightening up. He stood now with the palms of his hands braced against his kidneys and leaned back, stretching. Then he came upright again, keeping his hands in the same position. "Look like you could stand a dose of somethin' stronger than branch water."

McCanless couldn't help but smile at that. "I figgered you for a smart sawbones the minute I seen you."

McGee's chuckle was deep in his throat and chest, so deep in fact that it brought on a fit of coughing. He subsided into the red bandanna. Wiping vigorously, he crossed again to the cabinet and this time returned with a bottle of whiskey.

Doctor McGee poured generously into both tumblers. Then, touching the rim of his glass with his thumb and three fingers, keeping the little finger raised, he said, "It wasn't always I was a medicine man. Spent a number of years working the sober side of the bar, and that's about the best training a man can have who needs to know humans."

McCanless nodded. "Cards is better," he said. "But I allow you second on that." And he grinned.

Doc chuckled appreciatively. "You keep close to a man. I like that." Then, following a swift wiping of his nose with the red bandanna, he said, "To your good health, sir." And there was something in the way he said the words that caught McCanless.

"And to yours," he answered.

But neither drank. Both glasses stopped in midair as the same thought struck each of them. It was McCanless who said it aloud.

"To Wiley."

Doc nodded. "Wiley Hinges."

Later Doc had told him how Wiley had won the Circle Double O in a game of jacks-or-better from a cowboy whom O'Bannion had put up to buying the land in his own name, with O'Bannion money, and who had agreed to sell it back to O'Bannion, unbeknownst to anyone else, thus getting around any charges that the rancher was buying up all the land that he hadn't already stolen. But the damn fool had gone and lost it all to Wiley's three aces over kings.

"Wiley got himself right smack-dab into the middle of the cattle fight," McGee'd said. "Then the boys fighting O'Bannion, what's called the small cattlemen, or some call 'em maverickers, plus the council figured with Wiley marshal they'd be packing something extra. And I guess you know how Wiley liked the action. It all happened swift like a snake and there by golly was Marshal Wiley Hinges."

"Till some sonofabitch shot him in the back," McCanless had said, summing it.

"Nobody knows who actually done it," McGee told him. "Though for sure the Spade was back of it. Figgered they'd bust the small cattlemen by getting Wiley. Well, maybe they have." And his big hazel and red-streaked eyes fell onto McCanless. "Mebbe they have."

Now in his room at the Thermopolis House, McCanless stared up at the big yellow spot on the ceiling. Seven years, he was thinking. A lot happens in seven years. His chest itched, but he refused to scratch it. And now all at once he was at another kind of fire, or at least the remembrance of it as told him by Wiley Hinges, for actually, he still remembered nothing.

That day long ago when Wiley had found him in the smoking wreckage of the wagon train after Spotted Arrow and his braves had gotten through with it. How long ago? About eight he'd been; he didn't know for sure. Nor did Wiley. But leastways a button. The sole survivor. Wiley had come upon him kneeling by the bodies of a man and woman he took to be the boy's parents.

Wiley had told it to him later, a long time later, when he was like fourteen, maybe fifteen; in there. He had told him the whole of it, sparing nothing, for the boy had no recollection.

Wiley'd told him how he had been riding toward Star Canyon coming from Lead City when he'd spotted first the smoke and then the burning wagons. When the attackers had ridden off, he had come in, checking for survivors. There was only the boy.

The boy had not spoken a word. Wiley told him how he had just stared, not even crying. He hadn't moved when the man said to climb up behind him on the pony. When he had told him a second time and he still hadn't moved, Wiley'd leaned down and slapped him right across the face, hard. That hadn't done it, so he'd climbed off his horse and tied the boy across his saddle with rawhide and his lariat rope, all the time mightily concerned that some of Spotted Arrow's warriors could take a notion to return.

And the boy never spoke. For days he never spoke, didn't cry. Nothing. He barely ate. He just kept staring.

Wiley finally took him to a doctor in Lead City.

"Well, he don't speak," the doc had said.

"That is what I know for Christ sake, Doc."

McCanless always smiled to himself whenever he recollected the scene as Wiley told it; the stringy little doctor and Wiley standing hard over him, Wiley's hands on his hips, his long bony face listening to whatever sense the doc might come up with; a bit impatient as he tended to be, impatient with men who were slow to action. The doc, a ruminating sort of man, as Wiley had described him. Slow, ponderous, afraid to take a step; a man carrying a lot of worry, for, as Wiley had described him, he wore galluses *and* a belt to hold up his pants. And McCanless almost laughed aloud as he remembered the story, recollecting Clem Sayles that afternoon in the General Store, also a man with worry about his pants.

"What I am saying," the doctor had said patiently to Wiley, "is that maybe he don't want to speak. Maybe he just don't have anything to say."

"What'll I do then?"

"Give him time."

"Shit."

That hadn't satisfied Wiley, a man who did a lot of moving around; so while he built himself a smoke with his big bony fingers on those hands that could move fast as a striking rattler, he studied it and finally came up with a financial arrangement, leaving the boy with Doc; figuring he would more than likely do better in a home in one place than owlhooting on the trail, lifting a bank or a train, or hiding out someplace, or up all night with poker and now and then faro.

So Wiley had walked out of the doc's office. And this was how he told it to the boy when he was moving toward young manhood and speaking and doing things like everybody else. Wiley had gone down to the livery barn to get his horse and ride on out of Lead City. He had just cinched the sorrel, who more often than not swelled his belly so's you'd step into the stirrup and end up on the ground when that damn horse slackened and the saddle spun under his belly, when he felt someone behind him. And by God, there was the boy!

Wiley had tried giving him back to the doc, but the boy wouldn't. He just wouldn't; and he never said a word.

So finally, the way Wiley had told it, the upshot was he figured if folks saw him with a button maybe they wouldn't take him for such a owlhooter as they would otherwise, so maybe the deal wasn't so bad. Anyway, the end of the stick was he had him, and he raised him, Wiley did—from a button.

This good while it had been. And since Wiley knew everything and knowed he knew everything, as he himself put it, the boy had been educated real good, even at some place learning to read and write.

Then one day he was a man. And one day Wiley was gone. That day, when he was seventeen or thereabouts—he never knew his real age—Wiley told him it was time he cut it for himself. He, Wiley, was heading for Texas. The parting had been quick, the law having a hand in the decision, being there was a posse on Wiley's trail.

And Wiley had GTT, as the saying went—gone to Texas—leastways at first. While himself had GN—gone north—to Wyoming. McCanless; the name from a brand of plug tobacco Wiley had found at the massacre site, and used. And Finis, from a French sporting girl friend of Wiley's.

Sudden laughter in the corridor outside his room brought him to the present, to himself again, and he sat up on the bed. It was no cooler in the room. His body felt damp, and it seemed there wasn't even any air.

He had two things to do—find Wiley Hinges' killer and get his hands on some money. He would need money when he got to handling Wiley's spread, and right now he was down to small coins.

There was one place he knew always catered to people with loose mouths and loose money, a place where Wiley had given him considerable schooling.

McCanless stood up, still stripped, and just like any cowpoke, outlaw, or even lawman with savvy, the first thing he put on was his hat.

CHAPTER 5

When McCanless sat down in the chair vacated by the cattle buyer, the dealer broke out a new deck.

"It'll be straight draw," he announced, removing the joker.

The dealer was a small man named Three-Finger Titus, for the obvious reason that he had lost the fourth and little fingers on his left hand. But McCanless swiftly noted how he had developed his accident into a distinct advantage. Three-Finger Titus was unbelievably dexterous with the cards. And he was imperturbable, his black hair wet-looking, almost as though it had been pasted to his long head, his white shirt spotless, his very white fingers long, tapering at the nails.

It didn't take McCanless long to see what Three-Finger was up to. And why not? After all, card playing was a business; let the dudes beware. But McCanless knew his way with a deck of cards. Wiley had taught him. Mostly he had taught him that the main thing was to study the players. The players were the game. Just like gunfighting; a gun was a gun, but who was holding it was the question.

For a spell McCanless just drifted with the action, studying the other men at the table, their habits, their little giveaway comments and gestures. "You never find out about people meeting them in church," Wiley had told him. "And if you study poker you'll learn a lot about gunfighting." Over and over he had said it, said it to the point where his pupil had been sick of hearing it. But it had become a part of him.

Three-Finger Titus revealed his giveaway early in the game. Whenever he was bluffing he cleared his throat before taking a card or announcing his bet.

So far there hadn't been much spirit in the game. Three-Finger dealt skillfully, a ruby as large as his thumbnail sparkling on the little finger of his right hand.

A young Texas cowboy opened the pot and Three-Finger didn't stay. On the third deal McCanless opened for ten dollars, the usual, on a pair of aces. He was sitting to Three-Finger's right. The natty little dealer raised him twenty dollars. McCanless stayed and drew three cards.

Three-Finger's smooth face turned into a wicked smile. He cleared his throat and said, "I play these."

McCanless didn't help the aces. He knew what was coming, but he didn't know how much he would bet. Three-Finger glanced at McCanless' chips, calculating how much he had left. And then he bet fifty dollars.

McCanless pretended to hesitate. "I call," he said and spread his hand, face up, showing two aces.

Three-Finger could not conceal a look of utter disbelief. "I will be hornswaggled," he declared and threw his hand face down in the discards. "Didn't you know I stood pat?" he said in disgust. "How the hell can you call a pat hand on two aces?"

McCanless' smile was thin. "It was easy," he said, remembering how Three-Finger had cleared his throat.

Somebody ordered another round of drinks. McCanless was nursing his whiskey. He liked to drink, but not when playing cards. Drink led to carelessness. Wiley had drilled it into him that you had to know your own weaknesses as well as those of your opponents. "Keep a poker face," he had told him. "Keep silent. Don't complain when you lose a hand or spread yourself over winning one. Never drink while playing. Play tight whether it's cards or guns. It's all the same deal. Figure the odds."

To keep it friendly he took a sip of whiskey, his eyes searching the room. He didn't expect to see Gorm, but he might hear something of him. And too, he wanted to pick up anything he could on the Broken Spade and O'Bannion.

It was a big room. But the Buffalo Bar and Gambling Hall was not at all like the Elkhorn, where he and Wiley had spent so much time. There were no huge chandeliers holding coal oil lamps, no imported furniture, no thirty-foot mahogany bar brought all the way from Chicago. Here in Horsehead the appointments were indeed plainer, yet equally functional. The bar consisted of planks supported by upended crates. There was a large mirror in back of the bar, and alongside it a massive nude painting of a reclining lady. The liquor, McCanless noted, was passable; he had not yet sampled the food.

The Buffalo was lively, filled with smoke, the crash of laughter, swearing, the tinkle of the honky-tonk piano, and the smell of men. There were three monte tables, two wheels of fortune purring on the walls, as many poker games as the traffic could handle; and there were faro, dice, chuck-a-luck and other assorted means to facilitate the exchange of money.

A fat little drummer from Kansas City joined the game. His name was Tommy.

"Take a seat." Three-Finger Titus greeted him with a smile. Fat Tommy smiled back good-naturedly, taking the chair vacated by a government man who sold beef to the Indians.

There was another vacant chair suddenly, so McCanless got up from Three-Finger's side and took it. He knew that the little dealer was going to clean the drummer, and he wanted to be in a strategic position to win when he did.

Several rounds passed before his opportunity came. He was sitting to Three-Finger's left, and the drummer who was going to get taken sat to his right.

"Let's make it draw," Three-Finger said, picking up a new deck and again removing the joker. He dealt swiftly, his pale white hands looking chalky under the overhead lamp, the big ruby flashing with each movement.

McCanless passed. The next four players passed, making five in all. The drummer, the sixth player, opened with a ten-dollar bet. Three-Finger Titus came out with a twenty-dollar raise. McCanless called. Three-Finger showed no irritation at this, though McCanless knew he hadn't planned for more than one player to draw against him. The drummer called, which was according to Three-Finger's plan.

McCanless drew one card.

"Gonna win it, are ya?" Three-Finger said pleasantly.

McCanless didn't answer. He never talked while playing poker other than to announce his bet and the showdown.

Fat Tommy took three cards.

Three-Finger Titus said, "I play these," meaning he was standing pat.

The drummer, after a quick look at his cards, checked.

Without a moment's hesitation Three-Finger bet fifty dollars. McCanless took a card and raised him a hundred. He didn't have a thing, but Three-Finger had cleared his throat, and he knew he was bluffing again. He was sure Three-Finger was standing pat on a bust. Fat Tommy the drummer didn't matter, having checked. Even if he had helped his hand he would hesitate to call, with McCanless taking one card and raising.

The drummer showed his openers, two kings, and folded. Three-Finger shook his head sadly. "You lucky polecat," he said and threw in his hand. "Imagine drawing one card with all that money at stake."

McCanless tossed his hand in the discards and drew in the pot quickly.

One of the cowboys sitting across the table stood up and stretched. It was just at this point that a tall, spare man with a high forehead, wearing a gray broadcloth coat, stepped up to the table. "Mind if I join you gentlemen?" The accent was very British, the manners polished, the gesture of his hand refined. Obviously he was one of the multitude of English dudes flooding the West; hunting, investing money, buying up ranchland for companies in the East and in England. Not a popular group, McCanless reflected as he sized up the speaker.

The face was not one McCanless had noticed in the crowd of onlookers, or players at the other tables; and yet there was something familiar. Then he remembered he had seen the tall man standing at the bar, watching the game, evidently interested in something at their table.

"Have a seat." Three-Finger nodded to the empty chair opposite him.

"The name is Galston, gentlemen." There were a few nods; hands reached for drinks. The dealer shuffled the deck.

"Stud is the game; provided nobody objects."

"Stud it is," agreed Galston affably, taking out a thin cigar and lighting it.

The game opened high and fast with Galston and Three-Finger just edging out the first four pots evenly.

On the fifth hand McCanless dealt and Galston won on a full house. He also won the next round. Then Three-Finger Titus took a round, after which a cowpoke seated next to the Englishman won; and the next pot went to Galston. By now the table had attracted a crowd.

On the second round of the next hand McCanless, who was still dealing, had a jack showing. Somehow he felt this had to be the big pot, and he sensed the crowd was aware of it too. So far he had seen nothing in the manner of a giveaway about the Englishman. The man was ice. He spoke little, he sat still, smoking his cigar.

Galston had an ace exposed and bet $400. Everyone else dropped out, and when it was McCanless' turn he called and raised $400.

The Englishman was a smooth one, no question. He hardly touched his liquor. Only once did McCanless see even a spot of color in his face, when he cut the deck and pushed it back across the table. Now the players were totally silent as the game moved around the circle, with the crowd not missing a move.

Still, there had been something, McCanless told himself, something about the Englishman that he had seen, but it hadn't registered somehow.

Now Galston's crisp accent broke over the cards as he said, "I am a bit unhappy in taking advantage of you, Mister McCanless, but I have a pair of aces, and your jacks cannot beat me unless you catch another. How much do you have there?"

McCanless caught the thread of laughter and triumph in the man's voice, and then suddenly he saw it, that brief spot of color in Galston's cheeks, and remembered how it had been there when he cut the deck and passed it back for the deal.

By God, he was thinking, by God, that sonofabitch. But he knew this was the play where he was going to break into Horsehead one way or the other. He counted out his chips.

"Two thousand," he said, and without waiting for Galston to say anything he pushed the entire pile into the center of the table. He could feel more than hear the rustle of excitement that rose from the onlookers.

With the very slightest hesitation Galston matched it. He really seemed to have no nerves at all. But McCanless had seen him color—twice.

Galston's long face creased in an easy smile. "All right, sir. Deal the cards." And he turned his hole ace over to show that he was honest.

McCanless dealt the rest of the cards, and on the fifth round Wiley Hinges' "learning" paid off. He caught a third jack. All that Galston could come up with was a pair of aces.

The Britisher looked worse than sour as McCanless reached for the pot.

"Just a minute, McCanless." And McCanless noted the absence of the "mister" which Galston had been using all evening.

"Just a minute," the Englishman repeated, leaning forward in his chair. "That third jack was deep in the deck. I saw it flash when you riffled the cards, and I cut light."

"So you cut light," McCanless said, and suddenly his voice was as hard and even as a gun barrel. "You were taking an advantage in cutting light and the jack wasn't there where you thought it was." And he pulled in his winnings, keeping his eyes right on the other man.

Galston demanded to see the deck for an examination. "Since there are four jacks in the deck, and three landed in your hand, McCanless, there is then every reason to suppose the fourth jack cropped up." His voice purred with fury.

With no expression on his face, McCanless handed over the deck for Galston's inspection. The fourth jack was three cards from the bottom.

"That proves you slipped yourself the third jack," Galston said flatly.

There was an abrupt silence at the table, and for some wide area around the players. It was a long moment.

Now McCanless' words fell into that frozen tableau. "It proves only that you tried to bury the jack so it wouldn't crop up." And then he added one word, "mister."

He had dropped his hands beneath the table, feeling the onlookers drawing back, while he kept his eyes full and hard on the Englishman. A long moment passed while he watched it working in the other man's face.

Then McCanless, catching a slight movement of Galston's right hand, said, "I would not try that, mister. According to the rules and regulations I left my gun at the bar and you must've done the same. Except for that hide-out under your coat." He was watching the color come into Galston's face. "Better keep your hands still and on the table. I have got a derringer pointed right at your belly."

And in the stiff silence they all heard the ominous click of a gun hammer being cocked.

Three-Finger Titus suddenly sneezed. "Think I could wet my whistle a bit more," he said, and stood up.

Galston didn't move. "Very well," he said, and he dropped his eyes away from McCanless. "Very well. We will leave it. But we shall meet again, Mister McCanless." He stood up, turned on his heel, and walked out of the room, the crowd parting swiftly for his exit.

"Well, cowboy," Three-Finger Titus said, returning with a glass of whiskey. "You have made yourself one pretty powerful enemy there."

"You saw him bury that jack when he cut."

"I am telling you that Roderick Galston owns, or leastways represents, the Eastern and Prairie Cattle Company, what owns Cole O'Bannion's Broken Spade and God knows what all **else**, and he is no man to mess with."

McCanless moved back in his chair and brought his hands onto the table. He was holding two silver dollars between the fingers of each hand. While Three-Finger's jaw dropped open, he stood up and pocketed his winnings.

"And I ain't neither, Mister Titus."

CHAPTER 6

The first sunlight was just topping the distant rimrocks when he rode out to the cemetery. The graves were at the far end, away from the town, close to some juniper bushes. They lay side by side, with the markers simply telling the names and final dates. He wondered who had paid for the markers and the funeral. But it was good to be there alone.

He had taken off his hat and, holding it in his hand, he knelt on one knee by the graves, reading the inscriptions again; wondering what sort of woman Lillian had been, wondering too how Wiley had been those years since he had last seen him.

He could not imagine Wiley being other than the Wiley he'd known. It was hard to think of him married, settled, and siding the law.

McCanless stayed kneeling, he didn't know how long, while the light filled more of the sky, moving from behind the rimrocks and on down across the prairie toward the little town, the bright sun now washing into the juniper bushes beside him.

At length he stood up, still looking at the graves, wanting to say something to Wiley, but not having any words. Maybe later, he told himself. Maybe later when he had settled it. Then there might be something to say.

Stepping into the stirrup he swung his leg across the saddle and started out of the graveyard on his way to the Circle Double O at Box Elder Creek.

Now the heat was again in the land and he felt the trickle of sweat down the center of his back. The air wasn't any cooler as he topped the lip of a draw and looked down on the Circle Double O; a log cabin, a barn, horse corral, and a couple of sheds. McGee had told him the Broken Spade was using it as a line-camp since Wiley had supposedly sold it to O'Bannion. McCanless had said nothing about the deed and bill of sale Wiley had sent him. He would wait to play that card at the right time.

Now it was in the real heat of the day that he sat his horse and studied the layout below him. And there he saw a thin line of smoke rising from the chimney. Some-one was there in the ranch house. Maybe several? But he saw no horses anywhere outside. Indeed, no livestock at all, not even a dog. Of course there could be horses in the barn.

McCanless loosened the .45 in its holster and worked his fingers a little so they'd be limber. Then he started the dun down toward the ranch, quartering down the draw, in full view, but there was no other way of approaching. Wiley, he realized ruefully, would of course not have an outfit where someone could ride up on him unseen. All the way down the draw he watched for some sign of life. But there was nothing, only the thin string of smoke ris-ing from the chimney.

He rode right to the barn, dismounting on the side away from the house; painfully, taking care, not so much because it was painful still as because he didn't want to get hung up on some unnecessary move his recovering body couldn't yet allow. So he moved carefully. He ground-hitched the dun and moved swiftly and without sound around the barn to the door. He could easily be seen from the house should anyone take a notion to look.

There was one horse in the barn, chomping peacefully on a couple of forkfuls of hay in one of the stalls. He checked the rig—a low-cantled roping saddle, no rifle scabbard, and a stirrup length indicating someone about five feet five, even a shade less. No lariat, a pretty beat-up piece of leather all round. The headstall, which was hanging on a peg, was equally old. He was surprised to see a snaffle bit. Well, it wasn't any cowpoke for sure, and it wasn't a gunhawk. Although he wisely didn't rule out that last one completely. There were all kinds of professional killers. Everything pointed to maybe a kid horse wrangler, using some gear that'd been just lying around. The horse itself was about on the verge of being crow-bait, so he was equal to the rig. Well, maybe someone just came to sit a bit until things got to be more permanent, was how he summed it. Still, he did not rule out the possibility of weapons inside, and a trap.

He was therefore doubly on guard as he left the barn, making a wide circle to come up on the house on the side away from the barn. Still there was no sign of anyone. Not a sound from inside the cabin. He kept his hand close to the .45 as he approached the front door, easing along the wall of the cabin from the corner. The cabin's size indicated it might have three rooms including the kitchen where he calculated the chimney to be.

Now he stood to the side of the front door and again his eyes swept the terrain he had just ridden over, for an outrider could have let him through in order to come up on his rear. But nothing.

He placed his left hand on the wooden door latch. Bolted? Only one way to find out, and he drew the .45 with his other hand. He pushed up on the latch. It was tight. Then it gave. And in one swift movement he raised it, pushed open the door, without a sound, and stepped fast into the cabin, dodging out of the open target of the doorway.

His eyes swept the room. He was in the kitchen, facing

the range and, in front of that, a table at which a figure was sitting with its back to the door. Now the figure turned and a bowl fell clattering to the floor as McCanless raised the six-gun.

He found himself looking into the frightened face of a young woman. It was, in fact, the girl he had seen standing next to Doc McGee at the funeral.

McCanless was almost as surprised as she. He just slightly lowered the .45, watching the brightness in her eyes, the fear, and also the courage as she rose slowly to her feet and stood facing him. She was shaking some, but she wasn't giving any ground. Whoever she was, she had guts.

Quickly he scanned the room again, noting another door.

"Who's in there?" he demanded.

"Nobody."

"You sure!"

She nodded.

"Anyone else in the house?"

Again she shook her head, not speaking.

"Tell me straight," he said hard.

She had hold of herself, but still her breath came tight with the words. "Take a look if you want."

Swiftly he crossed to the door and kicked it open. It was a bedroom, and it was empty. He pointed the gun at her. "You go first into the other room."

She still didn't speak and he followed as she walked into what appeared to be a kind of parlor room, but with a cot in it as well as a table and chair.

He had noticed some articles in the bedroom that must be hers, and when they were back in the kitchen he said, "Who are you? What are you doing here?"

She stood facing him, her hands at her sides, staring right back at him, not defiant, but keeping her ground.

Then she said, "Who are you? I am minding my own business here. Who are you?"

McCanless did not show his reaction to that; he simply holstered the .45 and said, "This here's the Circle Double O, ain't it?"

"It is."

"My name is McCanless, miss; and this here is my property."

As he said those words all the color seemed to leave her face. Her eyes widened. "Wiley's friend!"

"That's what I am."

Her eyes brightened, and the color came back to her cheeks. She raised her hand to touch her mouth with her fingers, and suddenly he saw beauty in her.

"I saw you at the funeral. I didn't even think . . . I know Wiley wrote you." She took a step toward him. "I am Sandy Taggart, Lillian's sister. Wiley told me he wrote you, but I never knew if you got his letter or would come."

She moved suddenly to a chair and sat down, her hands in her lap, tears in her eyes as she looked at him.

"Got any jawbreaker?" he said.

"Coffee?" Suddenly her face cleared in a laugh. "That's what Wiley used to call it, jawbreaker."

He could think of nothing to say but, "You older or younger than your sister?"

"Lillian brought me up."

"Huh! Well, ain't that somethin'," he said, wagging his head, pulling a chair toward him with his foot, and sitting. "Wiley brought me up, too."

"He did?"

"From a button."

"But—you're not related. You're not his brother, or something."

"I am something; not his brother."

She looked at him for a moment and burst out laughing. "I like you, Mister McCanless. I like the way you don't mess with a lot of malarkey words."

He felt good then. He felt better than he had in this real good while, he told himself.

Then they sat there talking, while she told him how Cole O'Bannion had sold the Broken Spade to the Eastern and Prairie Cattle Company, how Wiley had won the Circle Double O and gotten to be marshal of Horsehead to boot, and that he'd been drygulched. All of which he knew from Doc McGee already. Yet coming from the girl it had a whole different flavor. Somehow, he could almost see it happening. It was history the way Doc had told it; the girl brought it to life, now and then through her tears and sometimes through her laughter.

Then she cooked up some mulligan, for by now it was getting to be nightfall.

"I was told this was a line-camp for the Broken Spade, being as they're saying Wiley sold it to them."

"That's what they're planning," Sandy told him. "But they haven't moved on it yet, and since I used to come out now and again to help Wiley, I just felt like staying out here a bit now. I will be leaving though."

He said nothing to that.

"I tried to get some hands to round up the stock. But no one would. They're afraid of the Spade."

"You ever hear of a man named Gorm?" he asked suddenly.

She thought a moment, then shook her head. He had asked McGee the same, and had been told he was one of O'Bannion's regulators; which he knew for a fact already.

After she had cleared the supper dishes she asked him how long he would stay; would he sell the ranch.

"First thing there's the stock to gather," McCanless said. "And I got to pay a visit to the Broken Spade."

He stood up.

"Better get some sleep," he said, and he realized she was watching the way he had moved his arm. "Hurt it some on my way from back home."

She said nothing.

"You better get some sleep," he said.

"What are you going to do?"

"Sleep."

"But tomorrow. What will you do tomorrow? I can help you gather the cattle."

"We'll see," he said. "We'll 'tend to tomorrow when it comes."

And he caught the brief little smile on her face.

She had offered him the bed in one of the other rooms, but he told her he would bed down right here in the kitchen.

"Won't it be more comfortable in a bed?" she said, her eyes on his wounded arm.

"That's what I know."

"Well, why not then?"

"I don't want to sleep too comfortable," he said. "That way I might end up sleeping a whole lot longer than I want to."

When she had gone into the other room he unrolled his bedding, blew out the lamp, and lay down. After a few minutes he got up, slipped out of the door, and took a turn around the corral and buildings. It was a clear night with a sickle moon, but there was no sign of visitors. When he returned to the house he waited a moment or two, then moved his bed to the other side of the room. He lay down on top of the bedroll, fully clothed and with his six-gun right near his reach. He lay there listening, thinking of Wiley and the Broken Spade; and now and again the girl.

CHAPTER 7

In the night the wind had risen. It was still dark when McCanless awakened. He lay there, listening. The only sounds to be heard were a part of the house. Now all at once he heard the rain. Soft. And once again he was back to the time Wiley had told him about, the time of the wagon train. He could remember only what Wiley had told him. The actual recollection, the life of it, again escaped him. It had always escaped him, no matter how hard he tried.

He got up now, and heard the girl moving in the bedroom almost at the moment he rose, as though she had been waiting. Then she came out into the kitchen and built a fire and began to boil up some coffee.

"I need some extra armaments," he told her.

"You mean, a gun?"

"Should be somethin' of Wiley's about."

She led him into the front room and, opening a chest, took out some old clothes to reveal a variety of guns that had belonged to Wiley Hinges.

And sure enough, there was that big blue navy Colt Wiley'd worn. It gave him a turn seeing that. But he didn't take it. Instead, he picked up a wicked-looking little scatter-gun.

He asked her about horses.

"There are about six head down in the breaks," she told him. "You'll surely find something good there in that bunch."

"Give the dun a rest," he said.

Later, he caught himself a little strawberry roan with four white stockings.

The rain was slackening, but still coming down soft as he rode out of the ranch, rode toward the Broken Spade. Reaching into his shirt pocket he brought out the makings and carefully built a smoke, not letting it get wet. While his thoughts went over his strategy.

He knew that his only chance was to work alone. No question about that anyway, since he'd always been a loner. Alone he could surprise, he could shock, he was maneuverable, he could improvise.

He had heard of the Eastern and Prairie, back in Cheyenne. It was one of the many big companies with eastern and very often foreign money buying up range in Wyoming, Kansas, Nebraska, and the Dakotas.

But O'Bannion running the Spade for them! That was a cute one. His own outfit. By God, that must truly gravel the man. O'Bannion, the big man in that part of the country, a man on the order of Goodnight and Shanghai Pierce and Matt Loving! Taking orders from a handkerchief bunch of English dudes, who never sat in a saddle, never touched a lariat rope or drank jawbreaker, who had no idea what a forty-and-found man did for a living. Only thing was, they carried the money.

Both McGee and Sandy had told him the war with the small cattlemen against the Spade and the Association and Eastern and Prairie had been going on a couple of years. No question, the appearance of a man such as Wiley had thrown a spoke into the Association. More than a few times Wiley had ordered Spade riders off his range, and then he had whipped O'Bannion's foreman, Harry Dime, and told O'Bannion he could go plumb to hell, making that man backwater as only Wiley knew how to do. McCanless grinned as he thought of how the Spade bunch must have taken the news that Wiley Hinges had pinned the marshal's star on his shirt.

McCanless spotted the rider off to his right just a short distance from the Broken Spade. And then another, sure enough, off to his left. Probably more out of sight. He knew they wanted him to see them. Figured to throw a scare. Dumb, they were. McCanless didn't give a damn. Let the whole outfit ride out to meet him. He had Wiley's scatter-gun lying across his saddle, just back of the pommel—why he favored that big old stock saddle with that extra space—with his slicker thrown over it. He was glad for the rain, for it excused a slicker like that.

"The secret," Wiley had told him a long time ago, "is never to try to figure too much on what's ahead. You got to plan—that's for sure—but you cannot worry it. For if you're all the time thinking about how you're going to get out, you'll never move in; you'll be done for. What I am meaning is that a man has to figger he is done for already, and then he is shut of that concern. Like you got nothing to lose."

It was this thought he was carrying with him as he rode up a long coulee and came right onto the Broken Spade. And as he came into full view of the ranch buildings and corral, a half-dozen riders closed in on him; they had been riding with him all along. They said nothing, only escorted him as he rode right up to the main building.

Now more men who had been in the barn and bunkhouse appeared. With the horsebackers there were about a dozen in all.

McCanless rode right up to the big house and sat the roan quietly, letting his glance rove around the faces of the men in front of him, feeling the presence of those behind. Now he swung around in his saddle and his eyes searched the group to his rear.

"Looking for somebody, McCanless?"

He swung back to face the speaker, moving the scatter-gun into a better position as he did so, but still keeping it under the slicker.

It was a man wearing a big white Stetson hat who had just stepped out of the main house. It was Harry Dime, Cole O'Bannion's foreman.

The rain had stopped now, and overhead the gray clouds were moving about swiftly as though preparing to clear away. But nobody at the Broken Spade noticed this. They all had their attention on McCanless and Harry Dime.

Now McCanless moved forward a little in his saddle. "I am looking for a little sonofabitch name of Gorm," he said. "My notion tells me he works for this here outfit."

"Never heard of him."

McCanless' hand was on the scatter-gun beneath the slicker, but he was leaning forward in the saddle as though he had a cramp.

"Then I have come to see Cole O'Bannion," McCanless said.

The man in the white hat said, "You can talk to me. I am foreman of the Broken Spade. The name is Dime. Harry Dime."

McCanless' finger was around the trigger of the scatter-gun. He spat over the roan's shoulder, squinting down at Harry Dime.

"I reckon you didn't hear me. I said I come here to see O'Bannion."

When he heard the movement behind him he said, "I have got this scatter-gun pointed right at your foreman's belly." And he let the slicker fall away for all to see.

He watched the color drop out of Dime's face while the foreman's eyes went instantly to the men in back of McCanless.

McCanless said, "You boys back of me, you ride

around in front here real easy, so's this thing don't go off."
He waited only a beat and then he said, "I mean right
now!"

When they were lined up in front of him, he said, "You
can all unbuckle." And when that was done, he said,
"Now you send someone to get O'Bannion." He was looking right at Harry Dime.

Harry Dime's mouth was a thin, tight line. His eyes
bore into the man on the strawberry roan horse.
"McCanless, you can't get away with this, goddam you!"

"Mister, I am getting away with it. Now send for
O'Bannion. I won't tell you a third time." And he motioned just slightly with the scatter-gun.

But before the messenger reached the door of the
house, it opened and a man appeared. He was big, solidly
built, with a gray head on which was a crisp brown Stetson hat; a man going on seventy.

"You wanted to see me, McCanless?"

"That's the size of it. Call your boys off and we'll talk,
'less you want them to hear what I have to say."

"I am not armed," O'Bannion said. "McCanless, you
can see that I am not armed."

"I am."

He waited for that to hit and then he said, "Tell them
to git. They can leave their hardware where it is."

Cole O'Bannion was a big man with a big face, and the
whole of his face reddened. But he nodded to Harry
Dime.

As the men started to move, McCanless said, "Me and
Mister O'Bannion will be in the house talking. I will have
him covered the whole time. Remember that." He was
watching Harry Dime, who was looking at the guns lying
on the ground.

O'Bannion was red with anger still, but he controlled

himself and said, "Come inside, McCanless. No sense being unfriendly. Nobody's going to harm you."

"That is what I know," McCanless said as he swung down from the roan.

"You have got that scatter-gun now, McCanless," Harry Dime said. "But next time, or the time after, you won't."

McCanless, who had been about to walk to the house, stopped. "You know somethin'? You are right. I might not have this scatter-gun with me next time or the time after." He waited a moment, while O'Bannion stood by the door of the house.

Then McCanless took a wooden lucifer out of his shirt pocket. "Here," he said to Harry Dime. "Stick that on that corral pole over there." And he added, "With the sulphur pointing up."

Reluctant, sneering and furious, the foreman did so, while all watched.

McCanless shifted the scatter-gun to his left hand. Now, pausing just a moment, letting all the breath go through his body, he dropped his right hand to the .45, drew, and fired.

"If any of you boys want a smoke," he said, dropping the .45 back into its holster, "there is fire on the end of that lucifer."

He took the scatter-gun in his right hand again. "We can go inside now, O'Bannion."

CHAPTER 8

Cole O'Bannion never carried a gun. O'Bannion understood a simple fact which Easterners invariably missed: that the western gunmen did not shoot important people, for the simple reason that such killing would invite severe retaliation. As tough cattle king John Chisum had put it: "Only half-wits and greenhorns pull down on a man of any substance." And Chisum, like Shanghai Pierce and a number of other big men, never carried a gun, even when he had vast sums of money on his person.

At the same time, O'Bannion, along with numerous others, remembered the former marshal of Abilene, Green River Tom Smith, who, though he never carried a gun, cleaned up tough Abilene with his powerful fists. But then one day this quiet, effective man was shot and killed while making an arrest; the villainy compounded by the brutality of his murderers' severing Smith's head from his body.

But now, while taking himself as an important person, Cole O'Bannion had no illusions that McCanless would necessarily follow John Chisum's dictum. And to be sure, McCanless was no greenhorn, half-wit, hard case, or gunswift. He was—something else. O'Bannion had heard of McCanless. He knew the type. Rare. Not the kind of man to be argued. Like Wiley Hinges.

And he had tried to get this across to that thickheaded Harry Dime. O'Bannion had put it to his foreman simply: "McCanless is no man to get previous with." And to make it all that much worse, those three idiots Dime had hired for security had done what they did out in the little box canyon.

He, O'Bannion, had really raked that knothead Gorm through the fire. "You goddam fool, you should never have let him get anywhere near Horsehead," was what he had told the sole survivor of that encounter, and he was including Harry Dime in his words. "You should have killed him, or left him be—one."

"But how were we to know . . . ?" Gorm had almost whined it.

"That is what the last corpse said," O'Bannion had snarled as he took a cigar out of his shirt pocket. He had lighted it, his big face etched in disgust and contempt as he surveyed his foreman and Gorm.

Blowing out a big cloud of smoke, he had said, "McCanless is not the kind of man you warn about something, you idiots!"

O'Bannion's disgust, however, was weighted with much more than the action of Harry Dime and the three regulators. There was the Company. The Eastern and Prairie wanted that section of land, the Hinges spread. And rightly so, he had to agree. For indeed, he had wanted the same range for himself. In fact, it was he himself who had put Ole Hanske up to getting that piece of land in the first place, then to selling it to him.

But meanwhile there had been the winter of the Great Blizzard, the Die-up when hell had visited the West and the cattle had been wiped out, and the ranchers too. And himself. Excepting he would recover. He had gone through plenty in his life and he would come back. Cole O'Bannion had fought and won through with the best of them. Hadn't he? Sure, maybe he wasn't as big as Chisum or the Slaughters—by God the land companies didn't push *them* around—but he'd made his mark. He'd fought his way up. Now, if he could just maneuver; maneuver and survive till an opening appeared.

For he felt there was a bust coming. The bottom was falling out of the market. But he, Cole O'Bannion, would survive. By God, he would. For he knew cattle. Always had. Since long ago, since Texas. Ah, those days.

Oh, he had seen it all. In those early years he could well recollect how a thousand head of cattle was considered a big herd, but then in the seventies the herds often grew to five, six thousand head. Yes, those days. Gone. Gone the time when he'd been a forty-and-found cowpoke, a trail boss, and yes, an owner. Hell, what did he own now? His saddle? His cigar?

No lick and a promise had it been in those bygone times. Nor was it even now. Hard work, and lonesome. That was the size of it. Funny, he caught himself thinking, how he was glad whensoever he heard those dire rumors about the bottom dropping out of the cattle market. Funny for a cattleman to think like that. Still, that could be his chance. If the market really crashed, he'd maybe get the Eastern and Prairie the hell off his back.

All of this was not thought out in detail as he walked with McCanless into the house, yet it was there, as it had been for some time now. It was behind everything he said and did, behind each gesture, behind the way he lighted his cigar, the way he offered one to a visitor. It was by now almost the whole of Cole O'Bannion, a man still vigorous in his later years, a man looking to maybe his last battle.

"Well, McCanless, what can I do for you?" And O'Bannion motioned to a chair with a rawhide seat, while he sat down in a leather armchair in front of his rolltop desk.

"I come by to tell you three things," McCanless said.

"I am listening."

"First, I know Gorm is on your payroll. I am going to find the little sonofabitch."

He said it blunt, putting the words at O'Bannion like the end of a long-handled shovel when you tamp around a fence post to harden the ground so it'll set. Short, strong, hard words, meant to stay right where he put them.

The rancher seemed not at all perturbed. "And . . . ?"

"I am taking over the Circle Double O."

Now there was reaction in the glint flicking into O'Bannion's eyes. The trace of a smile came as he spoke. "I should tell you that Wiley Hinges sold me his brand and all his stock, land, everything, just before he died. It is now part of the Broken Spade." He blew out a heavy cloud of cigar smoke, and looked at his cigar as he tapped the ash off the end so that it fell into the cuspidor alongside his desk. "I have got the bill of sale."

"I would like to see that. "

His host reached into the rolltop desk and extracted a white paper. "I have a copy," he said carefully. "In town."

McCanless scanned the document and handed it back. "It's a fake, O'Bannion."

"Can you prove that?"

"I have a bill of sale from Wiley Hinges dated a month earlier than that. He sold the Circle Double O to me."

"And I would like to see that document, McCanless." O'Bannion almost bit the words.

"Come on into town some time and take a look."

He watched it sink in, knowing that the rancher believed him; knowing he had to, since his own bill of sale was a fake.

"I will be riding over here in a day or two to gather any Circle Double O beeves might have strayed onto Broken Spade range."

He leaned forward in his chair now, with his forearms

along his thighs, his eyes tight on the rancher's face. "And finally, one thing, and it is this: I am going to find Wiley Hinges' killer."

The rancher, who looked away when McCanless spoke of the killing of Wiley Hinges, was just about to speak when suddenly a door at the other end of the room opened. And Roderick Galston walked in. He was wearing a dark blue broadcloth jacket, white riding breeches and highly polished black Wellington boots, English style.

"Ah, excuse me, O'Bannion, but I just wanted to say hello to my—er—card-playing acquaintance, Mister McCanless." The accent was even more clipped than it had been the other night, even more British—crisp, polished, carefully casual, smooth as a cup of tea in expensive china.

"That's all right, Galston," O'Bannion said gruffly. "We were just about finished, and I believe McCanless and his —uh—scatter-gun were just leaving."

The fact that he never looked at Galston while he spoke was not lost upon McCanless; and he did admire the rancher's recovery into a sense of humor about the scatter-gun.

Meanwhile, Galston had moved right into the middle of the room to where the two men were seated, and with a little bow of his curly-haired head said, "We haven't actually been formally introduced, and that's a pity. Sorry we got off to a bit of a wrong start the other evening. Anyhow, I am Roderick Galston and I am very glad to meet you." And with a little laugh he added the word, "Again."

McCanless nodded as Galston drew up a chair and sat down.

"I witnessed the little play outside a few moments ago," the Englishman continued. "I must say I did enjoy it." His voice was filled with his big smile.

Now Galston's eyes dropped to the .45 at McCanless' hip. "You are pretty fast with that hand weapon," he said. "And—uh—accurate." He laughed again. "Shooting that match. That wasn't bad. Not bad at all." Again the little laugh. "Pardon me, but I'm a bit of a pistoleer myself. Not in your class to be sure, but I have done some shooting back home and also on the continent. Target shooting mostly."

"Galston, you're hiding your light under a pack of fancy lingo," O'Bannion said. "Our guest will get the wrong notion about you." There was a dangerous look in the rancher's eye as he turned to McCanless. "Galston here is probably the best shot in the whole of Europe. He's got medals, silver cups; a whole mess of stuff to prove it."

Galston was holding up his hands in a gesture of extreme modesty. "You overdo it, O'Bannion. And actually, I am an amateur. McCanless there is a—uh—professional."

He beamed at McCanless. "Actually, I really love to hunt. I mean for the sport of it. I'll be getting up a deer and elk hunt in a few weeks. Perhaps you'd join me. Of course, buffalo is what I would really love to shoot. A few years back my late father bagged twenty-five hundred head when he hunted in Colorado. Some sort of record I believe." And his crisp laughter took over the whole room.

McCanless had been watching O'Bannion during the conversation, and he noted particularly the fact that the rancher did not join Galston's laughter.

"In any case, McCanless, I'd like to do some target shooting with you. I've set up a very good spot just a short distance from here, and I'd be happy to have you come on over and maybe teach me a few tricks."

Abruptly, McCanless got to his feet.

"I got work to do, O'Bannion. Remember what I said about them cows."

Galston had taken out a long thin cigar and was lighting it. Blowing out a cloud of smoke he said, "I mean that about the target shooting. I do hope you will accept my invitation."

McCanless had already started toward the door.

Turning at the threshold, he waited a moment, and then he said in a very quiet voice, "Mister Galston, I reckon I was brought up different than you. See, I only shoot a gun when I have to. I only shoot to kill."

CHAPTER 9

It was about the middle of the forenoon when McCanless and the strawberry roan rounded the cutbank and followed the trail down past the blue asters and shining goldenrod toward Horsehead. High above, a band of geese swung across the clear sky. Watching them he thought suddenly of the settlers still swarming through the West; still grabbing up land, putting up their sod huts or log cabins, measuring off section lines with a rag tied to a spoke of a wagon wheel, counting the turns, growing corn and beans and cutback wheat. The land was sure changing. Changing fast since the war, since the days of the Indian. Fencing all over the place. And sheep. So it was like Big Jaw Henrique had liked to put it back on the Sweetwater: "You know there is only one thing you kin do about it rainin'." "What's that, Big Jaw?" "Why, just let 'er rain."

Now he and the roan waded the ford just outside Horsehead, and he let his eyes scan ahead for any sign of possible trouble. He knew the word would be out that he was looking for Gorm. For a minute he wondered if maybe Gorm had left the country. But he was probably hiding out at the Spade.

He put thoughts of Gorm out of his mind. First things first. First he had to find Wiley's killer. And along with that he had to get the Circle Double O beeves back on their range, and that meant he had to rustle up some hands to help him, which was what he was doing at Horsehead in the first place.

And here was Horsehead, the little town suddenly springing up out of the prairie, sitting there like it had been blown from someplace and had just sat down like a clump of sage or soapweed in a twister, and stuck. The name of the town was carved into the wooden siding of the first saloon he came to, which happened to be the first building, punctuated generously with holes from bullets.

Horsehead, still pretty much an outpost and trading center for the Indian Territory, had moved more into the cattle trade in the past couple of years. There were the government men and the contractors, the sodbusters, and the ranchers, cattlemen and cowboys.

This year the cattle drives had started early, and all through May and June the prairie had been dotted with trail herds cropping the grass to the roots for miles around Horsehead.

The predicted boom had drawn not only many new buyers to crowd the town, but many hangers-on: the gamblers and prostitutes, the pimps and thieves, and the general hellers.

Now it was July and there was talk of the boom being a bust. All of which was running through the back of his mind as he started the roan up Main Street. The outskirts where he now was were surprisingly deserted, and he wondered why until suddenly a burst of firing up ahead threw a big spook into the roan and McCanless all at once remembered, even as his hand moved toward his sidearm, that, of course, it was the Fourth of July.

A band of kids raced suddenly across the street, dropping firecrackers right in front of horse and rider, and the roan spooked plenty then, but McCanless reined him and he pulled down into a high-stepping strut, snorting and whiffling and snaffling at his bit, with his ears whipping around.

So good, he reflected. Might be a likely time to corral a couple, three hands. Celebration time was always a time when you could find cowpokes who'd blown their last cent, though he didn't feel so sure anyone would want to go up against the Spade even so.

Just about all the residents of Horsehead, as well as nearby Tensleep, had come to see the parade, the minstrel show, the big prizefight. Posters were everywhere announcing the balloon ascension, the freaks and fire-eaters, and the marvel of the great Grimaldi's death-defying bicycle ride on a high wire strung across Main Street from the Thermopolis House to Sayles' General Store. And finally, the posters announced in the largest and boldest print of all, the Great Prizefight for the Championship of Herkimer County.

McCanless had missed the balloon ascension, but he had arrived just in time for the performance of the Great Grimaldi.

A big crowd had gathered to watch the Great One as he gracefully pedaled back and forth on the tightrope, high above the heads of the onlookers. The Great Grimaldi, veteran performer that he was, seemed not at all awed at being the center of attraction. He appeared absolutely at ease, his completely bald dome shining in the brilliant sunlight.

McCanless had been standing at the edge of the crowd, with a good view of the action, but now suddenly there was a distraction across the street. When he stepped up onto the boardwalk to get a better look, he saw two men bearing down swiftly on a man who was about to mount a big bay horse. Suddenly the man withdrew his foot from the stirrup, drew his six-gun, and fired. But the other two were quicker, and more accurate. The gunman, caught in the act of making off with horseflesh not his, was shot dead in his boots.

A scream rose from the crowd, but not because of the sudden death of a horse thief; rather because the Great

Grimaldi, himself attracted to the gun action below him, had suddenly lost his balance and had gone plunging to the street. He had the good fortune to land in a wagon box filled with sacks of flour, from which he rose with the breath knocked out of him so that he was totally unable to swear and could only emit coughing grunts. Dusted nearly white with flour, he had reaped a narrow escape. A cheer went up as he came to his knees in the wagon box. Moreover, the law had been maintained; a prospective horse stealer had paid the ultimate price.

While eager hands helped the Great Grimaldi step down from the flour wagon, a group of furious gamblers descended on him; they had bet heavily on his success. But for the moment, at any rate, their displeasure remained on the level of threats and name-calling. Others, exalted by the closeness of death or at least mangling of the high-wire artiste, swept him to the nearest saloon, only a few steps away.

Not wishing to leave the roan at a hitchrack where he would be exposed to firecrackers and other celebration high-jinks, McCanless rode him down to the livery stable. Following this, he too repaired to the saloon, where Grimaldi, still with a heavy amount of flour on his person, was arguing furiously with the promoter, who because of his fall was balking at paying him. Presently, the crowd around him began to drift away, and when McCanless approached he was nursing his irritation and injured vanity with booze.

He was a solid man, Grimaldi, broad-shouldered, but with the nimbleness of a professional dancer. He told McCanless that he had been born in a circus in Italy and had traveled all over the world with various troupes. He had been in Russia and Turkey, London and Paris; everywhere. He had performed before crowned heads. He was, he said, the world's greatest high-wire artiste. And he was

as good at telling a story as he was at walking or riding
the high wire. But he was worried about his pay and
about the gamblers who had lost money on him.

"Might be sensible for you to get out of town for a
spell," McCanless told him. "There's a lot of drinking,
and I've seen crowds turn nasty, specially when there's
money about."

Grimaldi touched the two ends of his waxed mustache
with his thumb and middle finger. He shrugged. But
McCanless saw that his words had hit him close.

"You think there could be trouble?"

"I am saying it might be good sense to lie low for a few
days."

"Ah, but where. They have not paid me. I have no
money." He drummed his fingers on the tabletop. "In
fact, my friend, I am expecting you to pay for my drinks."

McCanless liked that. The man acted in some ways like
a rabbit, but inside he was straight.

"I could use you."

"Use me?" Grimaldi's black eyebrows arched toward
his shiny dome. "What you mean?"

"I need a couple of good hands to help me out at my
outfit. Can you ride?"

"A bicycle, yes. A horse, no."

"But you know how to balance. You're pretty good . . ."

"Pretty good!" The Great One cut him right off.

"I mean, you're great; and so you could handle a horse,
is how I calculate."

"Why don't you get professional cowman for that?
There are lots here."

"They don't want it; they've all got jobs with their
herds."

"I think it over."

"I can learn you a good bit. Hell, Grimaldi, your bike is
busted all to hell, and you're broke. The promoter ain't

going to pay you and the gamblers are mad because you fell. I even heard one of them say you fell on purpose."

"Yes, I hear that sonofabitch!" The Great Grimaldi slammed his hand down on the table. "I take the job. I will be your cowboy. How much you pay?"

"Board and found; as for money we'll see what you know."

"Board and found?"

"A place to flop and your grub."

"I learn fast and you pay money?"

McCanless nodded.

The Great Grimaldi let a sigh flow from the top of his head all the way down through his body and out the bottoms of his feet. "Very well. So be it. But I must take thoughts before I accept the inevitable. It is my way."

"Drink up. I want to see the fight," McCanless said.

The fight was billed as "The Battle of the Century" for the Heavyweight Championship of Herkimer County. The gladiators were Country O'Toole, "former heavyweight champion of California," and Yankee Bill Blazes, "The Human Boxcar and challenger of John L. Sullivan and Jake Kilrain; a man as dangerous as a wild grizzly."

The fact that neither of the participants had ever trod foot in Herkimer County before that day was of no concern to the spectators. They had come to witness physical mayhem, and as long as the thrills were delivered, the fight billing was of no moment.

The referee was a wiry former stage driver by the name of Pony Whipple. Pony wore a waistcoat over his striped shirt even though it was a sweltering day, garters on his sleeves, a six-shooter at his hip. Beside the two fighters he looked like a pygmy, but it was swiftly seen by the crowd that Pony Whipple was running the show.

His voice was much bigger than his body and it carried

to the outskirts of the crowd, where many were standing on nearby roofs and the tops of porches.

After introducing the fighters he said, "You boys fight fair. No biting, no kicking, no gouging. No hitting below the belt. Lemme see those gloves. And mostly you do what I say. This here," and he patted the hogleg at his hip, "this here is the law. I shot a fighter last month up in Butte, Montana, tried to argue me. Just tellin' it so we don't have trouble. Now go to your corners and come out fightin'!"

These instructions were punctuated with a final and very liberal jet of saliva toward the side of the ring, which consisted of two ropes circling four posts on a raised platform. Pony looked down at the spectators. "They won't slip in that little bit of tobaccy," he said. "It's got too much spark to slither."

The ring, built specially for the occasion, was down by the cattle pens. The crowd pressed in, and Pony warned them back, his enormous voice charging into them like a locomotive. A number of spectators were standing on a flatcar on a siding, and some of them began to chant: "Pony boy, Pony boy, you're the one that we enjoy!"

As the two fighters went to their corners, the crowd's roar rose to a crescendo. Yankee Bill Blazes, really built like a boxcar, with not an ounce of extra flesh on him, moved around in his corner, limbering up. Country O'Toole, no less muscular, with hands like shovels, hitching up his trousers, appeared to be counting the spectators.

Someone hit a dishpan and the fight started. O'Toole rushed from his corner—seemingly intent on carrying "The Human Boxcar" right before him—to be met with a high, looping overhand right to the point of the jaw. The "former heavyweight champion of California" fell like a poleaxed steer, flat on his back and to all appearances dead to the world. A stunned silence covered the crowd while Yankee Bill Blazes waved his arms aloft in victory and Pony Whipple counted out the fallen gladiator, his right arm rising and falling like a scythe. But at the count of ten his right hand raced to his six-gun, while with his left he raised Yankee Bill's arm, proclaiming him the winner.

Bedlam instantly broke upon the unbelieving crowd. It was no longer a crowd, but a mob, as it surged to the ring, grabbing for the fighters. Pony fired his six-gun in the air and roared caution at them, but to no avail. Even he had to retreat before the onslaught of that great river of humanity, which screamed out cries of "fake," "fixed fight," "thievery," "kill the bastards." And now bullets cracked through the air. The ring ropes were ripped down, the platform charged, as the mob roared and beat its way to the two gladiators.

Still, Country O'Toole, supine on the ring floor, was not as dead or as dumb as he might have looked. At the first roar of the crowd he was on his feet in a trice and was running after the already departing Yankee Bill Blazes, who was almost halfway down Main Street. Yankee Bill raced into the Thermopolis House, where he had left his clothes; but Country, probably the more desperate of the two since it was pretty clear he had thrown the fight, ran like a deer straight to the livery stable.

"C'mon," McCanless shouted to Grimaldi. "Let's haul outta here. That crowd gets any uglier, they can turn on you, too." And they ran toward the livery stable to get McCanless' roan and a mount for Grimaldi if there was any left.

They had almost reached the livery ahead of the crowd when Country O'Toole burst out of the stable, ahorse and traveling at top speed. Bullets followed him as ineffectually as the crowd's curses.

The only trouble was he was riding McCanless' strawberry roan.

CHAPTER 10

"You have to get rid of him, O'Bannion. We need that range." It was Roderick Galston speaking.

The two men and Harry Dime were seated in O'Bannion's office. O'Bannion watched the pencil of sunlight as it wandered through the corner of the window and began to move slowly across the papers on his desk.

Without looking up O'Bannion said, "I know that. I don't need you to tell me that." He was irritated at Galston speaking to him like that in front of Harry Dime. Of late, the Englishman was becoming even more arrogant. And once again O'Bannion found his thoughts turning to how he could get back the Broken Spade; but he was cut short by Roderick Galston's voice.

"I mean that of course in, how shall I put it, in a financial sense. You know, O'Bannion, how the Company, and especially myself, deplores violence of any sort."

The look that O'Bannion turned on Galston made Harry Dime, who was watching, wince. It would have withered a rattlesnake, was how the foreman described it to himself later.

"You mean," O'Bannion said, "you want me to get rid of him. That's what you said. Only you don't want to be part of it; you don't want to get your hands dirty. But you want it done. I got you!" Reaching to his shirt pocket, the rancher brought out his second cigar of the meeting, and in one continuous angry movement, he bit off the end of it, spitting the little bullet of tobacco in the general direction of a cuspidor, and still in the same tempo, striking a match along the side of his fine California trousers. The lucifer sprang into flame and he puffed furiously on the cigar, releasing a great cloud of smoke into the room, while Galston looked on in disgust, his fine, aquiline nose wrinkling. And Harry Dime looked on in awe.

"I know that," O'Bannion repeated. His eyes swept to his tough little foreman. "Harry, I want you to send for Gorm and anybody else you'll need. He still out at the line-camp?"

"Right," Harry Dime said.

"But," O'Bannion continued, taking the cigar out of his mouth again and holding it between his thumb and the knuckle of his big forefinger, "this time no mistakes."

Harry Dime nodded quickly. "Right."

O'Bannion dropped his attention to his cigar ash for a moment and said, "I am meaning," and his eyes returned to his foreman, "that it has to be done right this time."

"Mister O'Bannion, it's like I told you. The boys had no notion who he was or what he was doin' in the country."

"Mister Dime." Roderick Galston brushed something off his elegantly trousered knee and leaned forward, with both elbows on his knees and with his fingers laced together in front of his chin. "Mister Dime, it is not that your men didn't know who it was and what he was doing in this part of the country, but rather that none of you realized that not only was this man coming to visit Wiley Hinges but that his name—his name, which would have been easy enough to find out—his name, I say, was Finis McCanless!" He sat back abruptly in his chair, slapping his thigh. "Damn it now! Try to see what I am telling you! McCanless!" Galston shook his head as though in awe at his own words. "My God," and his voice lowered almost to a whisper, "What bloody fools these mortals be!"

And a sharp, humorless laugh broke from beneath his sharply trimmed mustache. "You were holding in your hands, gentlemen, probably the most dangerous man in the whole of the West!"

The arm of O'Bannion's chair creaked under his weight as he leaned on it. "McCanless quit outlawin' this good while, Galston. He is retired." There was bitterness in the rancher's words, for he remembered the recent humiliation.

"A gunfighter never retires," Galston said, bringing in his rebuttal almost before O'Bannion was finished. He ran his fingers along the side of his jaw, then over his finely combed hair, then held them to his nose, smelling briefly the expensive cologne he had applied that morning. "Rather good that; a gunfighter never retires. Don't you think so, eh?" And he beamed at the two men.

"Let me get this here straight," said Harry Dime. "You want it so he never comes back here, or anywhere?" He emphasized the last word.

"Ah," murmured Galston, "a practical man in our midst." And he rubbed his hands together. Then his whole attitude, along with his hands, folded into a stern rigidity as he said, "I want it absolutely clear to both of you that I am completely against any violence. Is that understood? How you—uh—settle the problem, is of course your—uh—problem." And he smiled coldly.

The puzzlement on Harry Dime's face amused O'Bannion. "Just say yes, Harry."

"Do what you will," Galston said in a new voice. "But be smart about it."

O'Bannion felt something stir in the back of his neck as he looked into Galston's eyes. He had seen a lot in his time, a lot more than most, but he had seldom seen eyes and face as cold as what he was looking at right now.

Silence filled the room.

Then Galston spoke. "Handle it. I am delegating the job to you, O'Bannion. I shall hold you personally responsible. But you must understand—and I say it again—that neither I nor the company will tolerate the least suspicion of anything that is not according to law."

O'Bannion knocked the ash off his cigar and let his eyes move around the office. God, he was tired of Galston. But for the sake of expediency he put down his pride and said, "Don't worry about it." And turning to his foreman, he said, "It has to look right to the town. I don't want trouble with the council. Got it?" He had emphasized the "I" as he spoke.

"Got'cha." Harry Dime looked off into the middle distance, his thin brow wrinkling. "There is lots of accidents happen."

At his words Galston pushed both his hands in the foreman's direction as though not wanting to hear anything further, and stood up.

O'Bannion sniffed, leaned forward on one big knee, saying, "I don't care what happens, Harry, so long as myself and the Spade, and Galston and his partners ain't in the picture."

Harry Dime, realizing from the tone of his employer that his presence was no longer needed, rose to his feet and put on his hat, immediately feeling more at home.

When the door closed behind the foreman, Galston sighed. "Mister O'Bannion, there is something I want to say to you." And the rancher watched the half-amused light that had suddenly appeared in the Britisher's face. "I realize that you wish more than anything else in the world that you had not sold shares of the Broken Spade to my syndicate—controlling shares let me swiftly add—and that now you would do anything to, uh, rectify such a breach in what otherwise would be a quite independent life and career in the cattle business. But money is money." He released another sigh, a long one. "Money, as the old saying has it, is what makes the mare go. And you needed money. And need I say more?"

"That is done, Galston," O'Bannion said, and without even noticing it himself he cut his eye quickly to another door, one which led to a bedroom. "I am sticking to my part of the bargain. I expect you to stick to yours."

O'Bannion's swift glance to the door of his wife's room was caught by Galston, who now said, "You are missing my point. I am of course honoring our agreement. No question. What I am trying to get across to you is that we have to, we must, work together. Especially now with the headstrong McCanless in the picture." A little laugh broke from him. "Oh, mind you, I know about McCanless. I have heard a lot of him. At the Cheyenne Club last winter he was quite the subject of conversation. You know his part in the Johnson County war for instance, and some other things. He is no run-of-the-mill gunman; that is certain. But you and I have to work together." And suddenly his whole face lighted up, his young body seemed charged with vigor. "Agreed? Cole?" He laughed. "Cole. King Cole, how's that?"

And Cole O'Bannion, old curmudgeon that he was, couldn't help but smile too, for Galston did have a winning way about him.

"We will drink to it then," he said, and added with a chuckle, "Roderick." And his laughter grew as he said Galston's name to him for the first time, while something between them had become quite new. Bending, O'Bannion opened a drawer of the desk and brought up a bottle of whiskey and two glasses.

"A top brand, I presume," Galston said amiably as the rancher poured.

"You can drink all you want of this stuff," O'Bannion said, "and it'll never get you a headache built for a hoss."

He handed the tumbler to Galston. "Here, nose your way to the bottom of that. There is lots more."

"Here's to you," Galston said, raising his drink.

"To Cole and Roderick," O'Bannion said.

Galston joined his laughter, but he refused a second round. "Thank you; I'm not a drinking man really. But I am glad the fences between us are down now." He stood up. "I promised myself a little target practice this morning, and I'd better get to it."

O'Bannion smiled good-humoredly and waved his hand in a parting gesture as Roderick Galston left the room. He wasn't sure whether the animosity between them had lessened or become much more; but that was a fleeting impression. Cole O'Bannion was a tough old buzzard; he knew he hadn't survived this long in this country by being dumb.

When he was alone he walked to the window and looked out. The land swept to the distant foothills, with the high noon sun washing across. His land. The Broken Spade. But no longer. Not now. God. Goddammit to hell! He had built it; he had suffered it right out of the ground, by God. Fought the settlers, the sodbusters, the rustlers and outlaws. He'd even fought the Kiowa trying to charge him, trailherding through the territory. And he had gone through. Shot, clawed, punched his way through to build the biggest spread in the whole of that part of the country. The Broken Spade. Nothing had stopped him. By God!

Not even Millie had stopped him. Turning, his eyes fell to the picture standing on his desk. Smiling, happy Millie O'Bannion. Not now. Not this six years. He looked toward the door leading to the bedroom. Gone. Gone as a wife, she was. Paralyzed from the waist down after being thrown from that buckboard when the team spooked.

Nothing had helped. Not all the money. Not even the

best doctors in the country, from as far away as San Francisco and Boston. Still, he had not lost hope. He had never stopped hoping. Even when Myles had gone off to Texas—with the cards, the women, the whiskey too. Not a good son, Myles. He'd loved his son, but they had never seen eye to eye.

He, Cole O'Bannion, had stood it all. Alone. King Cole O'Bannion who'd ridden with Goodnight and Slaughter and Shang Pierce. Hell in a bucket. But he had been stopped. Yes—Millie had stopped him. His beautiful Millie lying there helpless. Only her eyes truly alive. She could barely speak, could hardly gesture with a hand, and from the waist down no movement at all. Only the eyes. Those beautiful eyes. And he had stood it, looking down into those eyes. Everyone had always said about King Cole that he was strong as they ever made 'em. But Cole O'Bannion knew very well it wasn't the weak who needed help and support; he knew all the way through him that it was the strong who were in the real need.

And then to top it, the winter of the big Die-up and the whole entire country frozen solid, with cattle and stock turned into blocks of ice. And those it hadn't wiped out, it had driven into the clutches of such as the Eastern and Prairie and the likes of Roderick Galston. Sonofabitch. I mean—God *damn* sonofabitch!

And so here now, here he was picking a fight with a goddam ex-outlaw and running his own outfit—what was and still should be his own—for a horse's ass bunch of English with a band of knotheaded regulators otherwise known as gunhawks so's he could just about keep his head above water and go on paying for Millie.

Suddenly he stabbed out his cigar—his third—in a plate he kept for the purpose and then threw the butt down hard into the big mouth of the cuspidor. He finished his drink and walked into the room where Millie lay in bed.

Cole O'Bannion stood very still beside his wife's bed. She was lying on her back, her eyes closed. Mrs. Weaver, who took care of her most of the time, had gone out for a moment. Millie's eyes were closed, and by the rhythm of her breathing he judged her to be asleep.

He stood for a long moment, not liking it, but at the same time not wanting to leave. And again he felt that little movement in his chest, and in back of his eyes and in his throat. He turned and walked out of the room.

He did not see, crossing to the door, that her eyes opened and followed him. He would never know how often she had followed him like that—with her eyes.

CHAPTER 11

A good while later that day when McCanless, followed by
Country O'Toole and the Great Grimaldi in a livery rig,
rode the roan into the Circle Double O, he was pleasantly
surprised to see Sandy Taggart standing in the doorway of
the house waving at them.

O'Toole had not proven himself as a horseman. The
roan which he had ridden out of the town livery had
taken him about two hundred yards down the street before throwing him. McCanless, in hot pursuit, had managed to grab the roan, mount him, and then had pulled
O'Toole up behind. Fortunately the crowd had been di-
verted by the quick thinking of Doc McGee, who, seeing
that massive destruction of life and property lay close at
hand, prevailed upon members of the town council to
start the balloon ascension for a second time. This diver-
sion proved successful, and McCanless and his two companions swiftly departed from Horsehead.

The livery rig he'd hired was all that was available in
the way of transportation, and even though the animal
was a crowbait, the two had their hands full. McCanless
did not look forward to getting any great amount of work
out of them.

"Unhitch him," he said, swinging down from his horse,
"and put him in the barn. You can leave the rig outside."
He led his own mount into the horse corral, stripped him,
and then walked into the kitchen.

"Dug up a couple of hands at Horsehead," he said.

Turning from the range, Sandy smiled. "Who are they? They don't look like cow people to me."

"One's a fighter, th'other's a circus man." He swung his leg high over the back of a chair and sat down. "No, they ain't much account with horses. But you takes what you gits is how you have to see it sometimes. Just like in cards. Got any coffee?"

"I put it on the moment I saw you."

He looked at her inquiringly, without speaking, and she said, "Nothing has happened out here."

"Thought you were moving back to town," he said.

"You said you needed help."

"Cowhands."

"You need a cook. And besides, I bet I can ride better than either of them."

A smile broke across his face at that. He was about to say something, but his attention was caught by a lock of her dark brown hair which had fallen down on her forehead.

Suddenly the door opened and in walked the Great Grimaldi. At sight of Sandy Taggart he changed in the wink of an eye from a rather bedraggled, almost out-of-breath individual to a perplexed, cautious, and polite man in his middle years. He straightened. He gave his mustache a twirl. His eyes, dull with frustration when he entered the kitchen, sprang to life. But then seeing McCanless, he realized he had come for a purpose.

"You got him stripped and in the barn, have you?" McCanless said, noting the changes going on in Grimaldi.

"Well, uh, not so exactly." Grimaldi threw a glance at Sandy's back as she lifted the stove lid and put in a stick of kindling. Then he turned back helplessly to McCanless, who was eyeing him with his head slightly canted to one side. "That horse. He don't want to stay in the barn. Though first he did. Then he change its mind."

"Meaning?"

"First he just took off when we tried to take his harness off."

"Took off?"

"Run right into barn before we unhitch."

"Wreckin' the whole rig, I'll allow," said McCanless, grim, as he got to his feet.

"Then he step on O'Toole's foot and he near kick yours truly in the head when I reach down to pick his halter rope or what you call it."

"Jesus," McCanless muttered, starting out of the house, Grimaldi following nimbly behind.

At the barn McCanless found Country O'Toole in a state of high agitation. The horse, a little black, had pulled the rig into one of the stalls, or at any rate had tried to, catching one of the shafts around a post, and was now trying to force his way toward the feedbox. But the harness held him to the rig, and he was getting more and more spooked, with the hames and lines falling down under his neck.

"Can't get next to him," O'Toole said. His chest was heaving and he limped. "That damn horse stepped on my foot. I am telling you he weighs a ton if he weighs a pound. Musta broke somethin'."

"You are lucky he didn't kick the hell out of the both of you," McCanless said.

The Great Grimaldi turned to O'Toole, whom he was beginning by now to see no longer as a rival entertainment attraction but as a fellow sufferer. He was about to speak, but McCanless cut him off.

"Go in the house and get some grub. Then we got work to do." He had already started toward the black pony.

"We hope it don't have to do with them animals,"

Grimaldi said, nodding toward the horse, who was showing more life than he'd probably shown in a couple of
years.

"It do," McCanless said, grim, as he began gentling the
animal. "You knocked hell outta this here rig. I'll have to
take it out of your pay if you ever start earning any."

O'Toole stopped at the door of the barn. "If. If! What
you mean if; you hired us!"

"I hired you on condition you'd be willing to learn. But
neither one of you knows a horse's head from his rear."

O'Toole turned to his new-found companion. "We
don't have to take that."

"Don't," McCanless said. "So where will you go? Back
to Horsehead? Them gamblers will more than likely run
you out of town in a feather overcoat."

The two stood dejected and silent. Then, turning
slowly, they walked out of the barn.

"Don't forget to limp," McCanless called after. And
O'Toole cussed.

In a few minutes McCanless followed them into the
kitchen. He sat down at the table facing them while
Sandy dished out the meal. "Hell," McCanless said. "You
boys never had it so good."

"What I need is sleep," said Country O'Toole. "That
was a tough fight with Yankee Bill; and I mean all that's
happened since."

"You got all winter to sleep," McCanless told him.

When they had finished, he took them back to the barn
and told Grimaldi to fork hay into the bin.

The high-wire artiste picked up the pitchfork toward
which McCanless had nodded, and stabbed it into a pile
of hay. A few wisps clung to the prongs as he withdrew it.
He tried again, with the same result. No matter how hard
or carefully he stuck the fork into the hay, when he drew
it out, expecting a forkful, he found only a few pieces.

"You got to feel for a solid place," McCanless told him, taking the fork. "Here." And to the amazement of the two of them he lifted a big load of hay on the fork in one thrust and carried it to the bin for the black to feed.

He showed them again, feeling with the round back of the prongs for a good place to pick up the load. "Try it." And he stood watching them.

"Something you got to learn," McCanless said when they were still not able. "It'll come. Hell, I shouldn't be feeding you two, you ought to be paying for me learnin' you."

The two searched his face for humor, but found none. And then suddenly Grimaldi picked up a small load of hay, beaming with delight.

"Good enough," McCanless said. "Keep learnin' it."

"Where did you find them?" Sandy asked later when they were alone.

"You should've come to the Fourth of July celebration," he said. And she laughed aloud as he told her about Grimaldi and O'Toole, about the horse thief and the prizefight, and their flight from town.

The next morning McCanless told his two hands to cut up some firewood for the stove. He had felled a fairly large tree and sawed logs into lengths that fit the kitchen range when split into kindling. Now he handed his two hired hands an axe and told them to get to it.

Standing inside the doorway of the barn, he watched Country O'Toole trying with all his might to split one of the drums from the tree. But to no avail. The axe kept getting stuck, or else it would simply bounce off the hard surface.

"You ain't doing it right," he said, walking over and taking the axe.

"I think I figure that is so," the fighter said sarcastically, his breath sawing hard from his efforts.

In a few swift strokes McCanless reduced the drum of wood to kindling. The two men watched in amazement while McCanless, not trying to split the block down the center, cut a slab off the outer edge; then quickly followed around the log, knocking off slabs by the stroke, until he had reached the core of the log. This he then split with a single blow of the axe. Kneeling down, he split the slabs into kindling sticks. The whole operation took about ten minutes.

"Didn't know cowboys ever worked like that," O'Toole said. "I mean, with their hands."

"It don't hurt to know everything," McCanless said, quoting Wiley.

"Bet'cha can't do that on horseback anyways," O'Toole mumbled.

"Shut up," said Grimaldi. "Or he have us do it."

In the days following, the education continued. He showed them how to catch a horse, how to make a rope halter, how to mount a horse bareback.

"Never move fast around a animal," he said. "You'll be liable to spook him. Talk to him. Gentle him."

One time, one of the ponies from Wiley's string turned his head to nip at him while he was cinching the saddle. McCanless without a moment's hesitation hit him on the nose hard with the back of his hand. "You let him get away with anything like that you're finished," he explained.

The following day Country O'Toole walked into the house with the knuckles of his left hand cut and bleeding.

"I did what you said, but he went and opened his mouth and I hit him in them big teeth."

"You'll learn," McCanless said, dour. But he looked over at Sandy and winked.

The girl marveled at his patience, the two green-horns at his devilish persistence and straight-faced humor, while McCanless marveled at the fact that two men—not one, but two—could have arrived at manhood years so downright helpless toward the real things of life.

Wiley's string were young stuff mostly, and pretty frisky. McCanless picked two mounts who looked a little less sparked than the others. Still, for the two dudes they were tough enough.

"He'll crow hop some when you get on him first, but you don't let him get his head down and you'll be all right."

"What'll happen if he gets his head down?"

"He'll start sunfishin' and you'll go ass over tea-kettle."

"Don't you have a gentler animal?"

"The Lord only made two kinds of hosses," McCanless said. "Them you can ride, and them you can't."

"We will take the first kind."

"Just remember the old cowboy song: 'There never was a hoss that couldn't be rode; there never was a cowboy couldn't be throwed.'"

He squinted at them from beneath the brim of his Stetson hat. "Hell, right now you got me in a hole on grub. You can't do nothin'. Can't handle a hoss, a axe, a pitchfork. Nothin'. Except talk."

"We are trying, Mister McCanless," the Great Grimaldi said, drawing into his dignity, which was considerable.

"I don't want you to try, I want you to do it."

Then one day the two of them managed to stay on their horses long enough and ably enough to ride out with him while he gathered a few head of cows. The boys were stiff and sore following their extended ride, but they were happy, proud of themselves.

"Cows have dropped their calves," McCanless told them that evening as they hunkered down outside the barn. There was a soft wind stirring and they could smell the grass and the horses. "Wiley's stuff is all mixed in with the Broken Spade herd. We are gonna have a helluva time cutting them out and figurin' which is our calves and which ain't. We got to start our gather right now 'fore the Spade starts throwin' their iron onto everything that moves. We got to get out there and check the mothers, then brand the calves. You got the picture of it?"

The two nodded. They were exhausted. Their hands were blistered, all their muscles ached.

"You don't learn horsebackin' and cowboyin' overnight," he told them. "Exceptin' that's what you two fellers got to do." And he told them they had only another couple, three days to learn it all. "After which we'll be ridin' over to Broken Spade range to gather our beeves."

One evening Sandy asked him why the two stayed. "They look as if they're ready to run away sometimes," she said.

"They stay on account of they are more afraid of me than the town or the Broken Spade, for the matter of that. I have been teaching them now to use six-gun and rifle. It helps keep them in line to be scared enough to know maybe they got to use 'em."

"Is it worth it?" she asked suddenly. She had been working around the range, and now she took off her apron and sat down at the table where he had been building a smoke.

"What do you mean is it worth it?"

"There'll be shooting. You will be shot at. And those two, they can't really defend themselves against professional gunmen." Color filled her face suddenly. "Isn't there any way you can—can talk with O'Bannion?"

He straightened his shoulders, reminded suddenly of his wound when she mentioned O'Bannion. He had almost forgotten the soreness in his chest, and the shoulder seemed as good as it had always been.

"It could get tough around this place," he said, looking at the side of her face. "Might make sense for you to pack along to town."

"I know you've been thinking that."

"Makes good sense."

"And you, you'll stay here till they come and shoot you," she said, and her words held the edge of bitterness. He had never heard her speak in that way.

"You got to do what you got to do," he said stubbornly.

And she was equally stubborn. "That is how I look at it."

He looked at the way she set her mouth, firm but not hard; and he even thought he saw a slight quiver.

Then she said, "You are not the only one who grieves for Wiley Hinges and, and for Lillian."

In the lengthening light of the evening coming into the kitchen, he got up and took the glass chimney off the lamp, preparing to light it. Out of the side of his eye he saw her run the back of her hand across her face and, in the light of the match, saw the glisten of tears which she was trying to rub away so he wouldn't see.

CHAPTER 12

McCanless was in the corral shoeing a little bay horse who was pretty spooky and didn't want to stand. He had him snubbed tight with his halter rope around one of the corral poles, and every few minutes he'd have to stop to gentle him.

Now he was just fitting the last shoe when his two cowhands rode in. He had already spotted them when they came splashing across Box Elder Creek, Country O'Toole on the big bay mare and the Great Grimaldi on the sorrel gelding. McCanless didn't look up at their approach, but kept right on working.

He was holding the bay's left rear leg across his lap, squatting, with his back to the animal, his eyes squinting against the smoke from the cigarette hanging from his lip, while the waning afternoon sun bore down on his back. All the while he kept up a gentle conversation with the bay, a soothing horse talk to hold the man-animal relationship. Years ago Wiley had told him, "It is like the both of you is doing something, not just you shoeing him or busting him, or whatever the business. That way, you'll learn, you get it done better."

"Easy, boy." The bay whiffled through his nose, his ears moving around at the approach of the riders. "Be still now. Be done directly." The bay stamped his left forefoot and pulled at the leg lying in McCanless' lap, almost upsetting him.

"Goddammit, stand still, I said!" The words were sharp

and there was irritation in the man's voice, but there was no violence; the contact between them was not broken. Now the bay nickered as the sorrel and bay mare came closer and their riders dismounted outside the corral.

"Keep them horses out of here," McCanless said, not looking up. "This here feller is a mite spooky." And he added, "I'm about done, anyways."

Without letting go of the bay's leg he reached down and picked up a new shoe. He had clipped and cleaned the hoof and rasped it to make it level so he could fit the shoe, which he now did. Then he let the foot down and, with the tongs, placed the new shoe in the fire which he had built only a few feet away.

While the shoe heated, he stretched; his chest was slightly sore again and his shoulder aching.

"Anybody get throwed today?"

A smile came to the two faces.

"Nope. We done just perfect," said Country O'Toole.

The Great Grimaldi swept his hands through the air. "We ride today like the champions." And he beamed.

McCanless took the cigarette from his lip and crunched it out between his thumb and forefinger. Now he brought out fresh makings from his shirt pocket and bent his attention to building a smoke while he questioned his two cowhands.

"What did you see?"

"Lots of cows."

"Broken Spade or Circle Double O?"

"Mostly Spade, but some Circle ones."

"Men?"

"About a dozen."

"What the hell d'you mean—about? How many men did you actually see?"

The two looked at each other in pain and surprise,

dropping from their high good spirits as their teacher brought them back to school.

"They was eleven, I do believe," O'Toole said. "I mean, they *wuz* eleven," he said, closing his eyes as he added it in his mind.

"They all together?"

"Four in two lots, and three," said Grimaldi. "They ride toward that big butte you show us that time."

"They carrying a lot of armament?"

"Nothing more than usual. Handguns, some long guns in their saddle scabbards."

McCanless bent his head. He was pleased at the way they were finally beginning to catch on. But he was sure not going to let them know it.

"If you boys don't learn right now to see things exact, you'll never leave this country on your two feet," he said. "They were Spade men, were they?"

Grimaldi nodded. "We were not sure; but they looked like it. Feller with a white hat riding with them."

"And a feller with a derby hat," O'Toole said. "Looked strange."

"Gray derby was it?"

Again they were thrown, but under his scrutiny it was not easy to lie. "Don't remember," Country O'Toole said.

"Did they see you?"

"They must of. They couldn't of helped but see us. But we just kept on riding. We didn't stop to socialize or anything."

McCanless took a deep breath and let it out slowly. He rolled the paper and tobacco together quickly, licked the open edge of the paper and gave it a final roll between his hard fingers. Then in one swift motion, he gave the cigarette a long lick and, twisting the end, put it between his lips.

He was silent now, turning it all over in his mind.

Gorm? It more than likely was Gorm; though there were those who wore derby hats on horseback. Still, it wasn't common. Now he picked up the tongs and lifted the iron horseshoe out of the fire. It was almost white hot. Raising it, he brought it close to his face, close enough for the cigarette to light. Then he put the shoe back in the fire.

"About ready." He was speaking, not to the two men, but to the bay horse. "Now you stand still and we'll get ourselves shut of this shoein'."

"Kin we help?" O'Toole asked.

"Watch."

He set the bay's leg on his lap again, squatting about halfway to the ground, and then he picked up the shoe with the tongs and dipped it in the bucket of water standing next to the fire. The steam, rising with a hiss, spooked the horse, but McCanless kept up his running conversation, almost losing his balance a couple of times as the bay moved. At last the horse stood still and McCanless fit the shoe. Seeing that it was a right fit, he dipped it in the water again. Now, holding nails in his mouth, he placed the shoe again and nailed it, hammering swiftly and clinching each nail. Then he clipped off the nail ends and rasped and buffed the hoof so that it was smooth. Finally he put linseed oil on the hoof as he had on the other three.

"Got yourself a new pair of shoes," he said, putting down the foot and straightening.

The bay nickered when McCanless rubbed him between his eyes on the big white splotch. And when the man turned away he pushed at his back with his nose.

"He likes you," Grimaldi said. "He is man's best friend."

"He is lookin' for some grub," McCanless said, and he began picking up his shoeing tools.

Squinting at the sun he said, "Let's see what the cook has rustled up for us."

When they had been at the table awhile McCanless said, "They will be all mixed in with the Spade's beeves, so we will have to go careful."

Sandy put down the coffee pot and sat. "Wiley got all his young ones branded," she said. "But I couldn't get any help to hold the herd after he was shot."

"Well, least he did get them under iron," McCanless pointed out. "And just in time it looks like." He looked across the table at Grimaldi and O'Toole. "Tomorrow morning we will start riding over the range and picking up our stuff, now that you young fellers know one end of a horse from the other. You know this brand. And you know the Spade. Anything looks like it's had a running iron put on it you let me know it right now."

"Isn't that hard to tell?" Sandy asked. And again he had the feeling that she was defending the two men, as though she felt he was too hard on them. But he told himself it was probably her mother instinct.

"Pretty tough, you're right. By now especially, with the hair grown over a good bit."

"Well, we are cowboys now whether we likes it or not," Country O'Toole said, and Sandy smiled at him.

McCanless said, "Not till you've learned to handle Indian river whiskey. That's the real test."

"What kind of whiskey?" Grimaldi asked. And Sandy laughed, for she had heard the story from Wiley.

"They make it along the Snake River," McCanless told them. "Only at a certain time of the year. Thing is, when a man has fought enough of that libation past his palate and has quietened the war in his guts, he becomes too drunk to sleep. You cannot even close your mouth after such a brew. The tongue—I have seen it myself—is twisted and weak and the throat is only a black hole."

Again Sandy broke into laughter, watching the expressions on the faces of the two men.

McCanless took his time in the telling. "The base is a barrel of water taken from the headwaters of the Snake when it is at flood, early spring, that is. The bigger foreign bodies are strained out and it is diluted with alcohol. Black tobacco is added and a twist or so of strychnine to give it kick. You add soft soap to make sure you've got a bead. It is then cooked over a slow fire. How do you test this savory brew?" He paused with one eye closed, looking at his listeners pensively with the other one. "You want to know?"

"How it is tested?"

McCanless nodded.

"How?"

"Best way is to throw in some elk hooves, and when they disintegrate the whiskey is just prime. Some folks use steer hooves, but that's not so sure," he added, with his face as straight as the back of a new playing card.

Sandy burst out laughing. "Would you like to try some?" And she glanced at McCanless, who winked at her.

"You mean, you got some of that stuff here, in this house?" Country O'Toole could hardly believe what he had heard.

Sandy went quickly out of the room and returned in a moment with a bottle of whiskey. "This isn't the real Indian river whiskey, but it will have to do."

"You are cowhands now," McCanless said, when Sandy had poured into four tumblers. "Whether you like it or not."

"By golly, this here looks like the best part of the deal," Country O'Toole said, lifting his glass, and the Great Grimaldi beamed at him.

When the Great Grimaldi broke out in a coughing fit

after taking too much on his first swallow, McCanless said, "Hell, if I can't kill you fellers one way, I will another."

That night as he lay on his bedroll, McCanless thought of the morrow and of finding Gorm. Somehow he felt that Gorm could lead him to Wiley's killer. Gorm would know; Gorm the regulator. For it must have been one or more of them who had done the bushwhacking. And Gorm would tell him. He would beat it out of him. And the thought came to him that Gorm—maybe Gorm—was the killer.

CHAPTER 13

Morning penetrated the valley's silence without breaking it. McCanless had been up in the dark, as was usual with him, and now as the tip of the rising sun reached above the rimrocks surrounding the great valley, he walked to the corral and checked the horses they would use that day. He had an uneasy feeling about something and he didn't know what. It wasn't long before he found out.

He had just finished checking the saddle rig and had walked out of the barn when he heard the approaching horseman. Swiftly he stepped inside the barn for the Winchester, which he kept cached in one of the stalls.

He stood now just inside the door and waited as the horse and rider broke from the stand of box elders and quartered down to the ranch. Early it was, real early for a rider to come to call. And he checked as far as his vision could reach to see if there was other unannounced company.

It was Roderick Galston who rode in, with the sunlight dazzling the silver conchas on his fine tooled saddle, and the silver butt of the sidearm at his hip.

The Englishman, McCanless noted, was not yet used to western style riding. He rolled and bounced in the roping saddle. His stirrups were too short, and he rode stiffly, now and again pumping up and down the way the English do on their little saddles. Yet for all that, he managed to handle his horse. McCanless noted the high polish on

his expensive Wellington boots reflecting the brilliant
sunlight as he rode right up to the barn.

"I wanted to have a word with you, McCanless."

McCanless canted his head some, squinting against the
sunlight now as the whole of the sun rose over the rimrocks. "Have you et yet?"

"I have had breakfast, thank you." The visitor smiled.
"You know, I do find western hospitality charming; the
custom of always offering food. So warm, that. Even to
someone you might not particularly like," saying the last
with a glint in his eye. "No, I'll not even dismount, but
will state my business."

"I am listening." And McCanless still kept a part of his
attention on the trees, which offered the best approach
for any sort of attack.

"I know that O'Bannion made an offer to Hinges for
the Circle Double O; and Hinges refused," Galston said.

"That is what I know."

"I thought I would repeat the offer." Galston gave a
quick smile as though he was handing out something.
"O'Bannion told me it would be a waste of time, but I
thought I might try anyway, and even sweeten the pot
somewhat."

But already McCanless was shaking his head. "Mister,
you could throw in the whole of the Broken Spade to me
and I wouldn't sell this spread. O'Bannion was right."

"You are sure you do have title?" Galston's face had
suddenly stilled.

"That is what I said."

"We can check the town files."

"Do that."

There was a flush on Galston's face now, but he controlled himself, taking a moment to find his usual compo-
sure. "McCanless, this will be your last chance."

"Maybe it is yours, Galston."

The Englishman shifted in his saddle, and McCanless thought, the dumb bell will have saddle sores by noon.

Galston leaned forward, his arms crossed on the pommel. He looked at the man, who had again moved slightly from his place away from the doorway, his eyes still checking the land behind his visitor.

"I admire you, McCanless. I don't mind saying so. It's really too unfortunate we are on opposite sides of the fence." Leaning back, he looked up at the sky, and then he leaned forward again. "The Eastern and Prairie could use a good man like yourself."

"So long, mister. I got work to do."

"Think it over. You could come to work for us. The pay would be attractive." He paused and then went on. "O'Bannion, you know, won't be around forever."

McCanless looked up at the rider. "Me an' my crew will be out gathering Circle stock. I am just telling you and you can tell your men case they see us." Then he said, "And mister, I expect to find the Circle Double O stock. All of it."

They remained on that last sentence for a long moment, their eyes holding one another, until at last the Englishman looked away.

"Very well then." Galston touched the tip of his hat with his forefinger and turned his mount. His eyes were on something at the other side of the stretch of ground that ran from the barn to a small shed.

"You must have grain in there," he said.

"That is one of them pack rats you're looking at," McCanless said.

"They're frisky buggers, aren't they." And suddenly, without any warning, as the pack rat darted across a band of sunlight, Galston drew his revolver and fired.

His bullet hit the rat dead center.

"Not bad," he observed, with a smile all over his face as he turned back to McCanless.

McCanless said nothing.

"We really must have that shooting match one of these days soon, McCanless. I mean, in spite of our differences." And he carefully returned his gun to its holster. "No, that wasn't bad at all," he continued, with the same smile, as McCanless still didn't speak. "Don't you think so?" And his smile grew even broader.

McCanless shifted his weight, now standing swing-hipped, with his thumbs hooked into his leather belt. "Not bad," he said. And then he added, "For a dude."

And he turned his back on Roderick Galston and started walking toward the house.

CHAPTER 14

The day was so hot the sound of the heat crackled in the trees, in the dry grass, and it hit a man in the face like limp leather. Everything was hot to the touch—the saddle horn, a man's thighs as they spread across his saddle, the butt of his handgun. The sun burned, it scorched; and for the three men of the Circle Double O there was no escaping it.

The Great Grimaldi and Country O'Toole had wrapped bandannas around their heads, beneath their hats, letting the cloth cover their necks and foreheads. But there was little relief.

"I feel my wrists burning," Grimaldi announced.

The horses moved slowly across the prairie, their coats sleek with sweat. Twice McCanless had ordered a dismount while they rested themselves and their animals. But by noon they had gathered quite a few head of Circle Double O stuff, mostly steers, but some she-stuff too, and calves. McCanless had to admit to himself that he felt good about it. And he even felt pretty fair about his two cowpokes.

The work was hard, but not too difficult. He had to teach them just about everything. Now and again he roped an animal out of a bunch of stock so he could check the brand real close for any running-iron work. But mostly they had little difficulty making the gather. And by late afternoon they were driving some fifty head toward the Circle Double O.

Of course they were watched, as he knew they would be. He had spotted the riders at the very beginning. Every so often one would show, just to make sure their presence was noted by McCanless and his crew.

On an impulse he had brought along Wiley's Deane & Adams, which had stood him in such good stead in the box canyon, and had slipped it into a holster which tied around his waist. Wearing a large shirt, he could keep the weapon well hidden.

They were driving across Willow Creek, not far from the ranch, though still out of sight, when the horsebackers came. They were twelve. And they were heavily armed, riding in hard and fast.

This time McCanless made no effort to throw down on the foreman. The Spade riders all had guns and rifles at the ready, and he was not interested in a massacre, no matter who survived.

"Pickin' a few head are you, McCanless?" The foreman looked even tighter than usual, as though he had been poured into his clothes.

"I am pickin' out Circle Double O stuff."

"Then maybe we'll just let the boys check it over."

Harry Dime had ridden right up close, with a man on either side of him; the others had fanned out a few paces back. It didn't look good to McCanless, no matter how it sliced, but it was the moment that had been coming; and he had chosen his ground.

"I don't see no derby hat in your bunch," he said.

"Derby hat?"

"Your pal Gorm. Where is the little sonofabitch?"

"He ain't, McCanless. He just ain't."

"I'll find him. He can't hide forever." He could feel the fear licking at Grimaldi and O'Toole, and for a moment he almost felt sorry for them. "How come you fellers are

so feared of three men?" he said to the Spade foreman. "I
mean, carrying all that armament."

"Just protecting Broken Spade interests, McCanless."
The foreman sat his horse, rigid from the top of his head
to his heels and toes.

"How come you wear galluses *and* a belt?" McCanless
said, and remembered Clem Sayles, whose skin was as
loose as Dime's was tight. "You ain't very sure about
them britches looks like, eh boys?" And he threw a look at
Grimaldi and O'Toole, but those two did not at all appreciate McCanless' effort to loosen them.

"This ain't a funning thing, McCanless." Harry Dime's
words were as hard as his eyes.

And now McCanless hardened. "Mister, you will not
find any Spade beef amongst them critters. And so I ad-
vise you and your men to get off Circle Double O range."

Harry Dime's sharp face broke into a hard laugh.
"Hear that, boys?" And the riders within earshot started
to laugh. "He tells us to get off our own range," the foreman went on. "Tellin' us to get off of Broken Spade
range."

McCanless was listening closely. He knew the buildup;
he knew what was coming. And he knew that in the tone
of voice would be revealed the moment of action. But he
was ready, and so was Wiley's Deane & Adams.

"Where is Gorm?" he said, bringing the little man up
again in order to throw Harry Dime off his pace.

"Gorm?" The foreman looked real innocent. "I just told
you, McCanless. Gorm ain't round. I don't know any
Gorm. Gorm? You sure you got the name right?"

"That is what I said."

"McCanless, let's drop it. Nobody here knows any
Gorm." And Harry Dime's face creased in a tight smile.
"There is twelve of us here, and I don't see no scatter-
gun."

"That is correct; no scatter-gun. But there is that little belly of yours right smack in front of me, and I do believe you know I'll get you even though your men cut me in two. I will still spill your guts all over that pretty little saddle."

"Mebbe." But the foreman's words were weak, his smile was only painted on his face.

"You are forgetting just one thing," McCanless said.

"And that is?"

"Me, I don't mind dying. On the other side of it, you mind a lot."

The foreman was silent. He was not without courage, Harry Dime; but he had seen McCanless light that wooden match.

The nine riders had finished their work of looking over the gather and now were moving in to where McCanless and his two hands and Harry Dime sat their horses.

"Find any Spade critters?" McCanless called out, not taking his eyes off the foreman.

Nobody said anything.

"I ast you somethin'."

"Nope," somebody called out.

"Then haul ass!" He moved his arm about an inch closer to his right hip, while the foreman's eyes flicked.

"Don't get nervous," McCanless said with an easy smile, while with his left hand he reached to his chin and scratched into his two-day stubble. But he knew the attention of Dime and his men was on the gun at his side.

"Just don't get any closer to that .45," Harry Dime said.

"Sure won't." And with the speed of a striking snake, his left hand dropped inside his shirt and came up with the Deane & Adams. "Hold it!" And that gun was pointing right at Harry Dime's life.

"I will be riding onto Spade range tomorrow for the rest of my beeves."

Harry Dime's eyes swept the ground behind McCanless and to the sides. "I got men to your right and left with Winchesters. And men right center back of you."

"That's what I know."

"So you'd trade yourself and your two men here for a bunch of critters."

"There is one way to find out."

Harry Dime said nothing.

"Now you can take your men and get off Circle Double O range."

The foreman suddenly looked toward Willow Creek, and his eyes squinted. Then without another word he turned his cow pony and his men followed after him at a fast canter.

McCanless nodded toward the cattle. "We'll bring them in closer, then catch us some grub."

O'Toole had sweat running on his face and Grimaldi's hands were shaking. Both looked about ready to fall out of their saddles.

"Mister McCanless," Country O'Toole managed to say after a moment. "I don't feel this job is good for my career."

"Why not?"

"You take too many risks with our lives; my life."

And Grimaldi nodded in swift agreement, his mouth hanging open.

Suddenly McCanless laughed. "Sorry I worried you." And then he was serious again. "I bin tryin' to teach you two fellers to see what's going on, but I don't have much success at it."

"But they could have wiped us out!" Grimaldi said, his eyes bugging out of his head.

"But they didn't."

"But you were as good as forcing them to shoot us."

"Except they didn't," McCanless insisted. "They

could've shot us all when they rode up. But they didn't. So Dime was just trying to backwater us."

"He was bluffing?"

"Yup."

"And you?" cried the incredulous O'Toole and Grimaldi in unison. "Were you bluffing?"

McCanless looked quietly at his two cowboys while he built himself a smoke. "I was not bluffing," he said. He struck the wooden match on his thumbnail and bent to the flame. "Never bluff," he said, straightening. "Never with a gun especially. If you bluff when you throw down on a man you are as good as dead."

His cowhands looked thoroughly at sea. "And does a man like Dime know that?"

"Course he knows. it. Exceptin' he knows I know it better."

And as they moved their horses toward the gather, Country O'Toole said, "There is a cloud of dust over yonder. I seen it a minute or two ago. By the creek."

McCanless looked wry at that, drawing rein and facing his two men. "They be riders," he said. "The prairie ain't so lonesome as those Spade boys first thought it was." He lifted his Stetson hat and resettled it on his head. And with a movement of his wrists on the reins he lifted his horse into a brisk gait, while calling back to Grimaldi and O'Toole. "You two bring in the gather. I got to meet our visitors. They are the town council and a few of the small cattlemen from hereabouts. Good thing they didn't get here any later."

CHAPTER 15

Cole O'Bannion listened carefully to the report from his foreman.

"I will get him next time," Harry Dime said.

O'Bannion shook his head. "No. There must not be a next time."

"If them riders hadn't come up it would've been different."

They were standing with Roderick Galston on the firing range the Englishman had set up for his target practice.

At this last remark of his foreman, a grim laugh fell from Cole O'Bannion. "And if the rabbit hadn't stopped to take a leak the tortoise wouldn't of beat him."

"You are right about there not being a next time," Galston said, almost overlapping O'Bannion. "We must settle this matter with McCanless once and for all. You must settle it," he emphasized, with his eyes on O'Bannion.

The rancher scowled, but said nothing.

Galston resumed. "He won't accept an offer to sell," and he ticked it off on his thumb and fingers. "He won't work with us; I offered him a perfectly good opportunity to be with the Eastern and Prairie. Oh yes," he added as he saw the incredulity on the faces of O'Bannion and Dime. "And, more than that, he resists the persuasiveness of twelve—count them, twelve—he-men of the great American wild and wooly West!" He shoved his hands into the pockets of his spotless California trousers.

"O'Bannion, the Company wants the Circle Double O. It needs it."

"I know that."

"Then get it!" Galston started to turn away. Then he stopped, and his voice was hard as he said, "Otherwise the Company—I—might find it necessary to reconsider our agreement with you. Do you understand me?"

Cole O'Bannion had turned gray with anger. In ashen silence he watched Roderick Galston stomp away. Still in silence, he and Harry Dime walked toward the house and entered his office.

"Sonofabitch," O'Bannion muttered as he stood in front of his desk. "Sonofabitch." The words were uttered more as prayer than imprecation; and Harry Dime heard them.

The silence deepened. Then O'Bannion reached into his rolltop desk and took out a box of cigars.

"What you going to do?" Harry Dime asked. And to his astonishment O'Bannion offered him a cigar, which he had never done in the long history of their association. The foreman accepted it with pleasure.

"How long have you been with me, Harry?"

The question was a second surprise.

"Fifteen years come the first snowfall. Thereabouts. Fifteen years." He wagged his head. "Yeah—fifteen . . ."

Both bit the ends off their cigars and lighted, each striking his own match. They smoked for a moment, each turning over in his mind something of the past fifteen years.

O'Bannion ended the silence. "Appears to me we got more gunmen than cowhands around this here outfit."

" 'pears so."

"You're the only one left of my old hands."

"Yup."

"I am a cowman, Harry. First and last." He spat suddenly into the cuspidor. "Or hell—I was. I used to be."

Harry Dime's eyes swept from the ash on his cigar to his boss. "Still are, far as I am concerned."

Cole O'Bannion's hand, holding his cigar, moved in deprecation. Then: "The men respect you, Harry. I can see that. Even those clowns we got now on the payroll. Fast with a gun maybe, but they can't cut even a half-assed bronc, and for sure not a one of them with the guts to back down a McCanless."

"McCanless, he is not ordinary . . ." Harry Dime started to say. But the rancher cut him off.

"He is tough. But we can out-tough him, Harry."

"How?"

"I got a notion." Cole O'Bannion reached again into the rolltop desk, and this time he brought out a bottle of whiskey. Uncorking, he poured with a swift accuracy admired by his foreman, bringing the brown liquid right to the edge of each shot glass without losing a drop.

"Man sometimes stomachs a lot," O'Bannion said, releasing a long whiskey sigh of satisfaction after downing. He nodded toward the closed door of the bedroom. "Mildred. You know what I mean."

The foreman nodded, the liquor quickly loosening his tongue. And his body. He looked quite different now. "It ain't like the old days. That is for certain."

"I mind the time we spent in Annie Holcomb's place." And there was merriment in O'Bannion's eyes which Harry Dime had not seen in this good while.

The little foreman grinned appreciatively at the recollection. "Best pleasurehouse in the whole of the damn territory," he said. I recollect that week I stayed—the whole of it, by God—with that cute little Lona Belle!"

"They don't make 'em like that anymore," O'Bannion sagely allowed, lowering his glass again with a gasp of pleasure.

And pouring once more, O'Bannion resumed his geniality with the man who had been his hired hand and fore-man for fifteen years.

Then Harry Dime returned to the origin of their meet-ing and suddenly said, "You got a way to get this goddam dude Company off of our backs, off of your back?" he amended. "You said you got a notion."

Cole O'Bannion began to nod pensively, though re-maining silent for a long moment. They had both seated themselves, and now the rancher sat, legs crossed with his right ankle on top of his left knee, leaning back in his chair, his elbow on the edge of the desk while his fingers turned his whiskey glass as he spoke. "You know me, Harry. I never worried about using guns when it was nec-essary. And I have seen it all. Been shot up myself more than a couple of times. But—this here is different."

"Different?"

"It's one thing packing a gun for your own spread. But for someone else? For this damn English outfit?" His face had darkened as he spoke and he ended by bringing his fist down on the desk.

Harry Dime watched in alarm as the two glasses of whiskey almost spilled.

"McCanless is a professional," O'Bannion said. "Harry, you are a top cowman, a top hand. You know how to use a gun but you ain't a professional gunslinger. Don't feel bad about him backwatering you. That's his business. He is a tough boy." He paused, his thick fingers drumming on the desk. "We have got to find somebody tougher. And before Galston does." He raised his shot glass and, hold-ing it at eye level, studied the light coming into the brown liquid. Then with a nod of his head he drank. "Thing is, see, Galston is going to bring everything he can to bear on this thing. Am I right? I mean, I see he wants me out of here, too. And more than likely yourself, to boot."

"Right." The foreman nodded, reluctant over the thought, but still seeing the fact.

"So we get somebody and we can handle it our way."

"Our way?"

A smile touched O'Bannion's mouth but it went no further. It was not in his eyes.

"Sometimes things can happen," he said softly. "I mean when there is a lot of action around. You never know. Thing is to keep things on the prod, moving fast; and keep right on top. Then—then you catch your opportunity."

Harry Dime's brow was creased with the effort to fathom what his boss was getting at, but O'Bannion, who had known him all those years, knew he was not long on thinking things through. He didn't mind, he knew Harry was loyal. That was what was needed. Loyalty. Because he was sure going to figure a way. The Spade should never, never had been sold to those damn Easterners and Britishers, the dudes. The Broken Spade was his; it belonged to Cole O'Bannion.

He watched Harry Dime's face clear, and then the foreman spoke. "So who is tougher than that sonofabitch McCanless?"

"Where is Gorm?" And the surprise on Dime's face brought a laugh right out of O'Bannion.

"He is out at the Tensleep line-camp." Harry Dime wagged his head. "But hell, he ain't anyone to go up against the likes of McCanless if that's what you're thinking."

O'Bannion's smile spread wide on his big face as he nodded. "That is true. He is not. He wouldn't last with McCanless the time it takes a dog to scratch hisself."

"We seen what happened to him and Bisbee and Kenny," Harry Dime said.

Cole O'Bannion was holding his cigar in front of him,

his eyes watching the long ash. Moving his arm to the side, he tapped the ash into the cuspidor near his foot. "No match for a McCanless at all," he said softly. And now his eyes were dead center on Harry Dime. "But there is his brother. His brother is another matter."

"Brother?" The foreman's eyebrows rose. "Gorm's got a brother?"

O'Bannion rocked back in his chair, his eyes still on his foreman. "Harry, you know me from old times. When have I ever hired a hand without I didn't know something about him?"

Harry Dime began to nod slowly as he let what O'Bannion had said move further into his thought. And all at once his face brightened. "I like to recollect hearing something about Gorm having a brother, or a cousin or something."

"But not just *a* brother, Harry," said O'Bannion reaching to the desk. "Gorman Tebeau has a special kind of brother." He was holding a newspaper clipping in his fingers. "I am sure you have heard of him." And his eyes dropped to the clipping and he read, "Cupid Tebeau, the famous Idaho outlaw, escapes from Laramie." He handed the clipping to his foreman and leaned back, enjoying the great surprise in Harry Dime's face as he read.

"You mean—you mean you'll hire Tebeau? Cupid Tebeau?"

But O'Bannion was already shaking his head. "No. No, Harry. That would not agree with Mr. Galston and Company policy of keeping everyone's hands clean. Now would it?"

"But what then?"

O'Bannion poured before answering. But he didn't drink. He said, "Let us say that McCanless, looking for the man who shot Wiley Hinges, finds him."

"You mean—Gorm."

"Who else?"

"It was Gorm," Harry Dime said. "We know that."

"McCanless doesn't know it. Yet." He reached to the desk and put his thumb and two fingers around his whiskey glass. "Harry, you can figure how Gorm's brother is going to feel when he gets the news that brother Gorman was shot and killed by a feller named McCanless."

Harry Dime's profanity was almost smothered in his excitement.

"You think it's a good plan?" O'Bannion asked.

"Hell yes."

"There is a better one," O'Bannion said. "It would be foolish to get Gorm killed unnecessarily. That is, for good insurance we might have the *both* Tebeaus coming at McCanless."

Harry Dime looked puzzled. "But you said something about McCanless killing Gorm and that would call in his brother?"

"Right. We'll let the news out that McCanless is gunning for Gorm; hasn't yet shot him. See, Gorm won't go up against McCanless alone, not after the other time at the box canyon. Then our friend from the Sweetwater will have to face Gorman *and* Cupid Tebeau. And we'll drink to that, by God!" They lifted their glasses high. And downed. And while Harry Dime was thinking how he would send someone for Gorm, and get the news to Gorm's brother, Cole O'Bannion was reflecting on how he would use the situation to get back the Broken Spade and settle his score with Roderick Galston.

CHAPTER 16

There were eight visitors come to call—four cattlemen, three town council members from Horsehead, including Mayor Turk Hinderman, and for some reason or other Doctor McGee; perhaps because he alone had any sort of acquaintance with McCanless.

Sandy had shown them into the front room and offered coffee. By the time McCanless rode up they had gotten more or less settled and some were even enjoying the hospitality.

He recognized some of the faces from the funeral service, but the only person he had spoken to beside Doc McGee was Councilman Clem Sayles, the storekeeper from whom he'd bought ammo. It was Sayles who did the introductions.

Doc McGee had started to speak, but Sayles, eager to take his place on the council, had cut in swiftly. There was, in fact, a certain nervousness since McCanless had entered. Mayor Hinderman now cleared his throat, preparing to say something immediately following the introductions, but at just that moment Clyde Greenbow of the Dot Box started off for the cattlemen.

"Thing is, McCanless, the Eastern and Prairie wants to buy up the whole of the country."

"Steal the country is the more like it!" snorted a man with white hair and a very red face. He was a rancher named Cy Skinner and he ran about three hundred head up on the eastern fork of Horse River.

Greenbow ignored the interruption. "When O'Bannion sold out to them it really opened it for a sweep through the whole of the valley and, in fact, the whole of the entire western part of the territory."

Clyde Greenbow was a tall, thin man with a long, thin nose and deep-socketed eyes. He spoke slowly, obviously a man who gave thought to his words before letting them out. "Us smaller outfits originally organized to protect ourselves against O'Bannion and the association of big outfits in the western territory. But mostly it got to be a fight with O'Bannion, him being the big spread in this country."

"But with the Eastern and Prairie coming in," cut in Mayor Hinderman, "we have all been hurting. I mean—bad." Hinderman, a man in his early fifties, was wearing a white shirt and holding a brand new Stetson hat with a crisp brim in his lap, as if it were a cake.

"But one thing we could say for O'Bannion is he couldn't help but sell," a councilman by name of Harley Sorensen put in. A somber-looking man, he spoke softly with a Scandinavian accent. Sorensen appeared well aligned with his twin professions: he was the town bootmaker and also the undertaker. He was gloomy, efficient, slow, lugubrious.

"Maybe you heard about Cole O'Bannion's wife, Mildred," Clem Sayles said. "Millie's from these parts; why some folks don't feel so hard on O'Bannion as some others do."

"I have heard," McCanless said.

"Thing is, we could of helped Cole." This from Skinner. "But he never said anything about letting in the Eastern and Prairie. That is what gravels me, and for the matter of that, most of us." Skinner's eyes searched for a place to spit. Finding none, he rose and walked to the door and opened it to emit a hefty stream of thick saliva.

"More feared of us than he was of Galston and his company, though that was back then," said another rancher, a man named Heavy John Jessup. "Thing is we would of wanted to keep others out of it. This here was our trouble, for us to settle. And we would have helped him against Eastern."

"It brought in the gunmen," a man who had not yet spoken summed up the trouble. "Whole valley is changed." The speaker was Little Phil Heizer of the Hammer and Nail, a middling spread just north of the Circle Double O near Crown Butte. Heizer, a man in his early sixties, looked brown as an Indian, and some in that part of the country claimed he had the blood in him. He was a top roper, and was always in demand during roundup.

Now Mayor Turk Hinderman spoke, holding his hand up to quiet Clem Sayles who was starting up again. "Maybe we ought to get to the real point of our coming here to see you, McCanless. I think you got the picture of what we're all facing here."

"What he is facing too," cut in Sayles, unable to keep out of it; and for his pains he received the mayor's dirty look.

Resuming, Hinderman said, "McCanless has got it pretty well straight, I'd say. Now, unless—Doc, you got anything to say? You ain't spoken yet." And he cocked his head at McGee, who had just been sitting in his chair chewing and listening.

"For a change, you mean—huh?" said Little Phil Heizer, with a laugh, and all joined in, Doc the loudest.

It was a good moment, the atmosphere of the room lightening considerably and easing into what was to come.

Turk Hinderman was still looking at McGee, who shook his head, his eyes smiling at the joke on himself, and so the mayor got to the point. "All I can say is I am sure that by now McCanless has figured out what we're after. We are needing a new marshal in Horsehead. And I do mean—need."

"Mostly just for the crisis," Doc McGee said, bringing it in smoothly. "Till the end of the season and the cattle drovers are gone; and when we hope to be settled with the Eastern and Prairie."

"How you mean settled!" said Skinner sternly. "Only settling with them kind is lead."

"Now, now Cyrus." It was Heavy John Jessup who brought the mollifying tone. "You know well as the rest of us that we are outgunned every which way you can shake a stick at."

"We had figgered Wiley would take care of things till the herds had shipped, leastways," Clem Sayles said.

"About the only time the cattle people and the town-folk and council agreed on a thing, I reckon," Harley Sorensen observed.

"Hell you care," Cy Skinner said, shaking his red face like a rooster. "You get the business both ways, by God."

"Cyrus—Cyrus." Little Phil's tone was chiding.

Harley Sorensen looked gloomily at the group. The aged story about the undertaker looking like he was measuring everyone for a coffin came to McCanless' mind as he watched him.

"Well, we are asking you to take the job," Heizer said. "That's the size of it."

"What d'you say, McCanless?" Clyde Greenbow leaned heavily into his words, trying to sum it up and get it set-tled. "Hell, you've took over Wiley's spread; why not the marshal job?" And his eyes swept the group with a wry humor. "We need you. And right now."

"Maybe he'd like to study on it," Doc said, looking at McCanless, who had not spoken.

"I just quit being a lawman up to Cohoes where I come

from," McCanless said. "I don't hanker for more of the same."

"Then you're out of a job and you can take this," said the mayor, ignoring his last remark. "McCanless, we need someone, I mean someone like yourself, and we need you right now." And he looked meaningfully at McGee.

Doc cleared his throat, sniffed, scratched under one armpit. "I don't know if you men realize how true that is, what Turk just said."

"What're you getting at?" asked Sayles, hearing something extra in McGee's voice.

"I am getting at some news I brought the mayor just 'fore we rode out here this P.M." And Doc was looking at McCanless.

McCanless was shaking his head. "Like I said, I am a cattleman now, not a lawman. I had enough of that line of work. The pay ain't all that great, and a man's too liable to catch lead poisoning."

Doc was still looking at McCanless. "You're looking for the man who bushwhacked Wiley Hinges, same as we are; only you got a extra reason. Am I right?"

McCanless nodded slowly, trying to catch what else he was hearing in McGee's voice.

"I believe I speak for all of us, that it's more than likely Gorm Tebeau did the job."

Now McCanless cut his eye fast at Doc McGee, the name striking him in a funny way. "Gorm? From the Spade?" And he remembered something he had felt about Gorm out at the box canyon.

"Yup."

"We got no proof on it," Clyde Greenbow said, "but it all points to Gorm. Wiley really backwatered him two, three times, and he did not take kindly to that."

"You said—Tebeau."

Doc sniffed. "I did." And now he said, "Gorm's brother

just broke out of Laramie. Maybe you have heard of his brother."

McCanless said, "I never knew Cupid Tebeau had a brother, and I sure never connected him with that little sonofabitch Gorm."

"They are brothers." McGee said the words with absolute finality.

"What's that to do with us?" asked Cy Skinner. "Gorm's brother breaking out of the pen?"

"It means," McCanless said, "that Cupid Tebeau will be heading for Horsehead Crossing."

"You know him." Doc said it as a statement.

"I know him. I know him from of old."

The room was suddenly silent. Sandy had left the men earlier so that they could feel free to talk their own way; and now, hearing the conversation stop, she put her head in the door to see whether anything was needed. But catching the feel of the room she withdrew quickly.

The silence lengthened with hardly anyone moving. Then McCanless pushed back his chair and stood up.

"I will take the job," he said.

CHAPTER 17

The question had been where he would make his fight. In the long moment of silence with his eight visitors, he had decided on the town, for the ranch was too exposed, open to easy ambush. In town he could control better. And moreover, Tebeau would catch a surprise finding he was also going up against the law.

Of course, no one could avoid a determined bush-whacking; but the town was a better place to flush Tebeau into the open. Even Wiley hadn't been able to keep himself covered at the ranch.

Sandy had told him how it happened, one evening when they were sitting alone in the house, Grimaldi and O'Toole having gone to their bedrolls exhausted from the day's work.

She had told how it had happened at suppertime, the time with Wiley. She had ridden out to the ranch that day to clean the house and sew some things for him as she now and again did, and he had asked her to stay for supper, as sometimes was their custom. They had finished the meal and were sitting talking. She always had liked listening to Wiley's stories and adventures.

They had only been sitting awhile after the meal when they heard the horses. Quickly Wiley had taken his Winchester and the scatter-gun and doused the kerosene lamps. In total darkness they had waited while the hooves beat closer.

At the moment just before they got to the house, Wiley

had slipped out the back of the building and had come up around one side just as the men brought their horses to a halt.

Inside the cabin Sandy heard a man call out. "Hinges! We want to talk to you!"

And then Wiley's voice came from a totally unexpected direction. "I have got you men covered. State your business fast!"

The man who had spoken now said, "We are making one last offer for you to sell. You better take it. Or else . . ."

"Or else what?" His voice had come from a new place, and Sandy had realized he was moving around so they couldn't target him.

"Or else you'll wish you had," a second voice from the riders had snarled.

McCanless had asked her if she recognized the voices. O'Bannion? Dime? But she didn't know them that well. She was not sure.

"The first speaker," she said, "was a big man. I looked through the kitchen window, and I think he had a beard. There was just a piece of the moon coming out at that moment that I looked."

McCanless wondered if it had been Bisbee. Certainly not Gorm, who was small.

Wiley had told them to git, and git right now or he would blast them right out of their saddles. He kept moving around as he spoke, so they never knew where he would be.

"He had told me to stay in the back room," Sandy explained. "But I sneaked into the kitchen and watched it all. It got to be lighter."

"You will hear from us, Hinges!" the big man had shouted.

It was then that Sandy recalled later she had felt they

were backing down too easily. But the thought slipped from her.

When Wiley came back into the house they both waited in the dark while the horsemen rode away from the ranch.

"Six of them," Wiley had told her. "Expect they'll try firing the place next time."

For several minutes they sat in silence, and at last Wiley got up and struck a match. He lighted one coal oil lamp and had just lifted the glass chimney on the second lamp on the kitchen table when there was the crash of breaking window glass and a shot rang out; and Wiley fell onto the table and slid to the floor.

Sandy had started toward him when a second shot rang into the room, smashing the one lighted lamp and stripping the room of light. In the darkness she had heard running steps, someone coughing, then a horse galloping away from the ranch.

Wiley was dead. She had stayed with his body all night, and in the morning had ridden to town for Doc McGee, who with Harley Sorensen had ridden out pronto.

McCanless had visited McGee and also Sorensen for details, but the story was essentially the same. A Winchester .44–.40 had done the job. Tracks were found outside the cabin, but they were not identifiable. As for the weapon, anyone could have in his possession such a rifle. The only thing McCanless got from McGee was that there had been a footprint near the window, indicating that the killer walked with either a limp or a slight stiffness in his right leg, and two empty shells. Not much to go on. Shells were shells. A limp, Doc had pointed out, if it was habitual might help identify the killer, but if it was just a sort of stiffness in the leg so that its owner came down harder on the outside of his foot, then it might not be chronic. It might be he was just stiff from standing out there a long time. What was clear, however, was that the killer had ridden in with the other riders, but had not left with them, the entire confrontation being a ruse. And it had worked.

McCanless didn't figure they would try another bushwhacking with him as target. It would be too obvious, trying for seconds, when everyone suspected Gorm. McGee had come up with the information that Gorm did in fact have a limp, but it had only been temporary from a pulled muscle. And it was in his right leg. Not enough evidence to make a serious charge; but that plus the fact of Wiley's backwatering him those times added to something, at least in a number of minds.

Of course, as McCanless knew Cupid Tebeau, he wouldn't go the usual way; he was not at all predictable. He was a mean sonofabitch killer, and there was nothing he would stop short of doing. Always Tebeau had wanted things his way. And this, in fact, was his weakness; which had gotten him shot up that time by McCanless, and then taken by the posse and stuck into Laramie.

No, he reflected again, the sensible place to confront Tebeau and brother Gorm was in town. And as town marshal. Tebeau against the law. With two of them to go against, McCanless knew he needed help. His choice had been made for the battleground. But what about the time? That would have to be taken as it appeared.

Tebeau. Sharp featured. A black mustache. Black eyes. And jet black hair under a black hat. High shoulders and long hands. Swift as the wind with a gun. And dead center with his bullets. That time at Elbow Creek, he'd just greased his shots into that posse, knocking half of them right out of their saddles.

The only one who could rein down Tebeau had been Wiley. Wiley, the leader of the gang. Tebeau didn't like that at all, but he went along. Only it was always a challenge; Tebeau was always looking for an opening to take over, to best Wiley, but Wiley was always one or two ahead of him.

The gang had been highly mobile, the personnel changing a good bit and Tebeau coming and going, along with Ace Cummings, John Clarke File, and some others with reputations.

Cupid Tebeau, tall, saturnine, had never taken orders well from Wiley Hinges. He was surly, sarcastic. But it hadn't been Wiley who'd finally called him, though everyone had been looking for it to come to that. Everyone knew that one day it would be Wiley Hinges and Cupid Tebeau going for grease.

But no. It had been McCanless.

The time, a late afternoon in March. The place, Ed Reeves' saloon at Pitchfork Junction. A half dozen of the gang had met to discuss the next job, and to divide the loot from the last. Spring, but still cold with winter yet in the ground, though the trees were awakening, the ground starting to soften some. Yet, animals and men were still moving in their winter tempo, still bundling against the cold, even if it was less; the horses and rest of the stock were still in their winter coats.

In Reeves' saloon the men circled the potbellied stove; the low-ceilinged room thick with the haze of smoke, the smell of heavy clothing.

"By God, you could strike a match on this here air!" somebody had said, and had drawn desultory laughter.

"Where is Hinges?" Tebeau had wanted to know.

"He will be here," McCanless had said. He was just reaching his young manhood then, and was considered by all but Tebeau to be Wiley's lieutenant.

"If he don't get here soon, sonny, we will have to get on to business without him." And Tebeau sneered and

spat angrily on the floor, not even attempting to hit a spittoon.

"How we going to divide the money without Wiley
when it is him has got it in his saddlebags?" asked Jelly
Jorgensen.

"We will divide it right now, if we get the wish of it!"
said Tebeau, his eyes flashing, his lip twitching so that his
mustache gave little jerks as he spoke. "And when Hinges
comes he can donate his share to us!"

Tebeau was glaring at McCanless as he spoke, as
though daring Wiley through him.

"We can wait, Tebeau, we can wait." It was big Ed
Reeves, who was part of the gang, talking. Big Ed often
took the role of peacemaker.

But Tebeau wasn't having any. "Don't argue me,
Reeves. I don't like the way this here outfit is run and I
am saying so!"

"Then why not tell Wiley?" McCanless said suddenly,
all at once feeling the devil in him as he did sometimes.

And then the room was silent. Something in his tone of
voice had called Tebeau, and the men knew it.

"Because I am telling you, sonny." There was no mis-
taking the sneer in his voice as he said "sonny."

McCanless remembered Wiley telling him something
about Tebeau, and now, just like his devilishness, it
popped into his mind and onto his tongue.

"Have you got anything else to say?" he asked. And
then he added, "Algernon."

Tebeau turned a dark red.

"Do not call me that. Nobody calls me that."

"Your mother did, I bin told."

"McCanless, he's too fast," Jelly Jorgensen said. "Let it
drop."

The sneer on Tebeau's face deepened. "Hinges ain't
here to protect you now, kid."

"We can drop it," McCanless had said, not afraid but realizing the foolishness they were getting into.

"Sonny thinks he's a second Hinges." Tebeau's face was still red with anger. "Well, maybe he is—another Hinges, bigmouthed and scared."

In the next moment they heard the horse beating up to the building. The door was suddenly flung open and Wiley strode in.

"That damn posse is right on top of us. Let's hit leather!"

McCanless in that second saw Tebeau's hand sweep to his holster. His own hand dropped to his side and brought up his weapon in one liquid flow. His aim was true.

Cupid Tebeau clutched his wounded arm, his six-gun dropping to the floor, his face twisted in pain.

"Mount up!" shouted Wiley. "'Less you want a rope necktie."

They were already racing to their horses. Tebeau bellowed in pain and fury.

"Get in a saddle," Wiley shouted to him. "Those boys are carrying longarms." And Wiley raced to his mount and spurred off, McCanless right behind him.

Tebeau had missed his stirrup and fallen flat on his face. Looking back, seeing Tebeau struggling to his feet, McCanless pulled his horse around and raced back.

"Get up behind me," he shouted.

But Tebeau managed to mount his own horse and the two of them now raced after Wiley and the others. Then, just as they were splashing through a creek about a mile from Reeves' place, the posse shot Tebeau's horse from under him. McCanless only just made it into the timberline to escape with the rest of the gang.

It was a close one, a real close one. But that kind were the best. They would all remember it. And mostly that day had shown the speed and accuracy and the cool guts of the boy Wiley Hinges had raised to a man.

CHAPTER 18

And so Cupid Tebeau had been taken and had retired into Laramie, vowing—the news swift in reaching McCanless—vengeance. And then, God, what a coincidence, his younger brother at Horsehead; sent, very likely, to take care of Wiley. And it was especially strange that he and Gorman Tebeau had met without either knowing the other.

Clearly, Gorm had come to Horsehead for the express purpose of killing Wiley, and the Broken Spade had fitted right in with his plan, and vice versa. McCanless would be dealt with by Cupid Tebeau personally. And Cupid—born Algernon Eustace Tebeau—was now on his way to Horsehead to achieve his purpose.

He had told Sandy the pertinent facts, what was necessary for her to know.

"Then you must get some deputies," she had insisted. "You can't fight them alone."

"I have got them two," he said, meaning Country O'Toole and the Great Grimaldi.

"They're more hindrance than help, much as I like them," she said. "Oh, I'm sure you can get some deputies who will really be able to help you."

He shrugged. "About as much chance gettin' deputies as there was hiring cowhands, case you disremember that."

"Can't the council get some people?"

"Who? Who wants to be a lawman in a town where

Cupid Tebeau and his kid brother are comin' in to kill the marshal?" He began building a smoke, while he continued. "So they carve 'hero' on your gravestone. As for money, it's enough maybe to buy a widow a mourning outfit."

She had made a picnic lunch on Sunday and they had ridden together to a place above the timberline that she had known since she was little.

He had not really wanted to take the time off, and yet he had surely wanted to be with her. At the same time, he knew he must stay loose and not get tight about what was coming. It was good to take a little holiday just for that reason. Getting tight about Tebeau and brother Gorm wouldn't help a thing.

He had told her some of his background, something of how Wiley had found him and raised him.

"And you still don't remember anything of what happened? You still don't remember your parents?"

He shook his head. "I guess I figure, like Wiley always said, that it don't rightly matter. What's of account is what's going on now."

"It might be nice to know who your parents were," Sandy said gently.

"On the other side," he pointed out wryly, "it might not."

They were seated on a little knoll high up, near the rimrocks, over a sweep of valley land and a lake. She had brought biscuits, jam, some eggs, and cold hotcakes made with hominy. They were both hungry, and while they ate they talked and looked at the valley. It was a soft, clear day, and they could see for a long distance.

"Strange they left you, the warriors. I mean, why didn't they either kill you or take you with them?"

"I used to wonder that sometimes."

"Know what I've been thinking?"

He grinned suddenly. He had been leaning back with his legs outstretched and with his weight supported on his elbows; and now he rolled onto one elbow to look at her, lying flat on her back, her eyes watching the top of the sky. "You bin thinking of me," he said. "How handsome and . . ."

"Come on now." And she sat up suddenly, clasping her hands around her drawn-up knees, her laughter fresh in the high air. "I'm serious. Have you ever thought that maybe you weren't a part of that wagon train, that those bodies maybe were not your parents?"

"It's a thought."

"Maybe you had different parents. Maybe you were captured earlier and you'd been living with the tribe, and then they took that chance to leave you there at the wagon train. Something like that."

"Mebbe." It had occurred to him before, but he had not dwelled on it. When he was younger he had wondered a lot about his parents, and where he had come from. Wiley hadn't been able to help him, and so after a while the questions had simply died.

There had been one thing that had stuck. Wiley had told him that he had never cried. All that time he didn't speak, he hadn't cried at all. And even later he hadn't cried. He had never heard of a child not crying. Not a white child, leastways.

"Maybe you're Indian," Sandy said suddenly, speaking the very thought that was in his mind, and had often been. "Maybe you were captured when you were a baby and they raised you like an Indian, as one of them, and then for some reason they brought you back to the white people like that."

"Might be." He had looked at that himself a few times over the years; not so much recently. There seemed no way of finding out. And he even wondered if it mattered. He didn't want to dwell on it. For there were times for deep thoughts and there were times for action. This time now was for action.

"Better get on back," he said. "I got to git on into town; get things corralled a bit."

She began collecting the picnic things. "You'll try to get deputies?"

He nodded as they stood together for a moment, looking once more at the valley. Then, holding the picnic bundle in one hand, he held her hand with his other as they walked to the horses.

When he had tied the sack onto his saddle, he turned and faced her.

"What will you do when it's all settled?" she asked him. "When you've settled all the things—Wiley's outfit, the Broken Spade, and Tebeau?"

And he caught the unsteadiness in her voice.

"Don't rightly know," he answered, speaking slowly. "I won't know what I'll be like when all that is over and done with. So how can a man say ahead like that?"

He was looking down at the toe of his boot, his hands just inside the tops of his hip pockets, his thoughts on what they'd been speaking of a moment before.

"Don't matter what a man was," he said, a little surprised at himself. "It matters what he is." And he added, "It's when a man's got himself, that's what he is and it's where he is."

He turned his head and looked directly at her. She was smiling at him.

"Yes," she said. "Oh, yes."

They rode back to the ranch without saying anything more. Inside him he felt something fresh and new. He was glad he had spoken to her like that.

CHAPTER 19

Roderick Galston was looking forward to his elk hunt. He had planned it carefully, had hired the top scout in that part of the country, had engaged a cadre of retainers to make sure the hunt would run smoothly. He had only one real regret, that his hunt would not equal in scale those his father had enjoyed.

Of course, it was not to be expected. All his life he had felt he could never measure up to his father. Indeed, in only one area had he surpassed the elder Galston, and that was in pistol marksmanship; albeit Sir Donan Galston had scorned the weapon, so there was never any contest. Yet in Europe, Roderick had proven himself peerless in pistol target competition.

Nor was Roderick Galston the total stranger to the American West that many people supposed. As a boy, a youngest son, he had accompanied his eminent father on a part of his great hunt in the untamed Colorado country of the early fifties. Possibly it was from this experience that Roderick gained his devotion to firearms along with his contempt for animal life. At any rate, it had set a style for him, even though he had not matched it, and had marked his youthful character.

Sir Donan Galston, international sportsman and heir to vast estates and wealth in the Old Country, had a blazing passion for the hunt. Westerners found his approach unorthodox. The actual hunt itself—tracking, patiently waiting for game to appear, reading sign, suffering the weather, fatigue, the arduous routine of the trail and the discomforts of camp life—formed no part of Sir Donan's concern. His retainers took care of all that; Sir Donan was simply transported in unique comfort from one hunting site to the next. For his sole interest was the kill.

On the buffalo hunt that young Roderick attended, Sir Donan had brought with him a retinue of gunbearers, bushbeaters, hunting dogs, and general retainers for such matters as reloading, skinning game, moving camp.

Arrived at the place of confrontation with the buffalo, the men built a shooting blind overlooking a draw. In this a comfortable camp chair was placed, and in front of it a stout forked stick was pounded into the ground. Young Roderick had watched fascinated while his father settled himself in the chair and rested his rifle barrel in the fork of the stick, while to his rear gunbearers stood ready with additional rifles.

As the herd, driven by the beaters and the excited dogs, came rumbling through the draw, Sir Donan sat in his easy chair and blazed away.

He would fire, drop the rifle to the ground, and grab another from a gunbearer to fire again. It was hard to miss. When the last of the decimated herd had suffered through the great blast, Sir Donan ceased fire. At this point, the retainers sprang forward to finish off the wounded with knives and tomahawks. Only the heads and hides of the animals were taken as trophies. The carcasses were left on the prairie to rot; Sir Donan no more deigning to skin the hides than he had even considered loading a single rifle.

Roderick planned his elk hunt on a considerably more modest scale than his father's, which yielded twenty-five hundred buffalo, more than fifteen hundred elk and deer, plus numerous bear and more birds and small game than he ever counted in his three-year hunt through the territory. Roderick, of course, had not attended during the whole of that time, but he had had a taste of it. Nor could he ever compete financially with his father. He was by no means poor, but he could not have afforded such an expedition as Sir Donan's; moreover, there were few buffalo now, and the elk and deer were scarcer than twenty years ago, owing in no small part to Sir Donan's efforts.

Though he loved to hunt, Roderick was actually more interested in pistoleering, and in the manipulation of men and money. Thus, he had risen quickly in the Eastern and Prairie Cattle Company. Shortly, he expected to take over the entire operation, a stroke which would fall the moment he settled this business of the Broken Spade and the Circle Double O.

So he had returned to America after almost a twenty-year absence, to find many changes. Land was less available. There were fences. There was the law. But here he felt he could reveal his true talents. He could operate within the law, using the law. Thus, he had used O'Bannion to gain the 200,000 acres of the Broken Spade. And he would acquire more. It was high time for O'Bannion to depart. He had only kept him on as manager after the takeover out of pity regarding his wife. But in this world there was no room for that sort of thing. A man such as McCanless understood that point of view. O'Bannion had bungled the situation with the Circle Double O; he was resentful, disrespectful. So he was certainly dispensable.

Few things surprised Roderick Galston, but he had to admit that the news of McCanless accepting the job of marshal of Horsehead did catch him off guard. He would never have considered a man like McCanless—at least as he had appraised him—would side with the law.

McCanless was too rough-cut, too free swinging, too independent to follow a book of rules. Unless—unless of course he had an ulterior motive.

.

And independent was how Galston liked to see himself, as a matter of fact. Unique. An original, as he described himself to himself. And it rankled him mightily to see the qualities he ascribed so highly to himself so obvious in McCanless—that freebooting gunslinger.

He had at first fully expected the man to sell him the Circle Double O; though that had been before he realized the nature of his relationship with Wiley Hinges. Still, he could not see him settling down on a ranch mothering a couple of hundred head of beeves. Even the marshal's job made more sense than that for such a man.

To be sure, there wasn't all that much difference—especially these days—between the lawman and the outlaw. A tin badge. And there were certainly those who wore the badge for extra reasons. For instance, Plummer up in Alder Gulch in Montana. Sheriff of the whole territory, including all the gold settlements, and by damn he had been running the bandits the whole while, planning robberies, holdups, killings. Over a hundred killings by the Plummer gang in one year, he had been told. Until he got caught by the vigilantes and hanged.

Was that McCanless' game? Using the star as a front for banditry; like Plummer? Like Hendry Brown, too, down in Kansas, who ran the outlaws while cleaning up the town and playing the honest citizen. Because McCanless certainly wouldn't be getting rich just wearing a badge, there was no advantage in being marshal of Horsehead. He would only be exposing himself to what the the Westerners called "lead colic." Clearly then, McCanless must have taken the marshal job for the same reason as Hinges; he was siding the maverickers against the Association, and they were probably giving him extra money. Thus, in actuality he was breaking the law, for it was against the law to brand mavericks. By damn! And yet was it that? Hell take it! It was another reason for his disliking the man so much; you just couldn't figure him out.

And finally, his ableness with a gun. Galston had never drawn on another man. He had never been in a gunfight. Yet, he had imagined it. He knew he had a fast draw, and he was surely accurate, having won top prizes in England, France, Germany, and other European countries as well as in the eastern United States. He had often imagined himself in a pistol battle. He wondered more and more what the real thing would be like.

Unquestionably one needed nerves that were reliable. Like in a poker game. Well, he had seen the way McCanless played poker—up close. And he had seen him light that wooden match out at the Spade. He had heard stories about him as well, stories told at the Cheyenne Club. The only man, it seemed, who had been close to his ability was Wiley Hinges.

And then one morning, passing outside the open door of O'Bannion's office, Galston quite accidentally heard the name Cupid Tebeau. And he realized that there was another with that ability, a man who might be even better.

CHAPTER 20

"I don't like that shoulder." Doc McGee took a cigar from the row of three in his waistcoat pocket and pointed it at his patient.

"What do you mean you don't like it?" McCanless, at McGee's insistence, had come to be looked over.

"I mean I don't like it. It's stiffening. When I move it you hurt. I can tell. I could tell when we were out at the ranch with the others."

"Did you say anything?"

"No."

"Good enough."

"But I see it hurtin' you, and I know it will get stiffer and could be real trouble."

McCanless snorted. "Course it hurts! Why should I pretend it don't!"

"So what are you going to do about it?" Doc McGee bit the end off his cigar and struck a match.

"What can I do?"

"You can rest it. What I told you in the first place. Course you didn't. Nobody listens to Doc. And you especially don't. So more sooner than later you will end up with it stiffer'n a board."

"Man's got work to do he's got to get about."

"But I told you to rest it, or it will not mend. Not only it won't mend, it'll get worse and you won't have use of it at all."

"Rest, huh? Just like that." McCanless shook his head slowly from side to side, as if McGee were crazy.

The doctor nodded, his expression sour. "That is what I am telling you."

"Want me to tell that to Cupid Tebeau and that sweet little brother of his?"

"Listen." Doc stood hard as a rock right in front of his stubborn patient. "I want you to rest!" He said the last word loud. "And why didn't you speak up about that shoulder being so sore when you were asked to be marshal?"

McCanless did not answer. He walked to the window of the little office and stood looking down into the street, one story below. It was just past noon and the town was drowsy. He watched a black and white spotted dog ambling across the rutted street, only just getting out of the way of a hay wagon pulled by a team of somnolent bays.

"I believe I told all of you I didn't want it," McCanless said presently. "You kin recollect that, I know. But not a one of you would have it. You all insisted." He kept his eyes tight on the street while he spoke to McGee, standing across the room behind him.

"Hell man, how many deputies you figuring on?"

"None."

"None!" The word exploded around Doc's cigar, which in the next instant he removed from his mouth.

"None."

"There has got to be someone. You know that; there has got to be some deputies helping you."

"You know better. Who is going up against not only the Broken Spade and the Eastern and Prairie, but Cupid Tebeau?"

"Then why in hell did you take the job! You said you didn't want it. Why did you take it!"

McCanless didn't answer for a moment, and then he

spoke softly, so softly Doc almost didn't hear him. "I didn't take the job," he said. "It took me."

"What in hell does that mean!"

"It means Cupid Tebeau."

Doc took a while to digest that, and there followed a silence.

"You know Tebeau then. You are saying that is why you took the job."

McCanless suddenly turned away from the window and faced McGee. "I know him."

"Then you know the odds. There will be two of them."

"I know the odds."

"They tell me you're a smart poker player," McGee said. "Then you know that when you're on the short end of the odds your best bet is to cut your losses and get out of the game."

A thin smile touched McCanless' mouth. "I also know that a good poker player doesn't play the cards, he plays the people," McCanless said.

Doc cut himself a soft smile at that. Then he said, "I will speak to the council. See what they can do about getting deputies. Hell, they owe me some things from now and again. They can raise the pay maybe, leastways till this thing blows over."

"Might as well spit into the wind," McCanless said. "But good luck to you."

"Then you will just be a sitting target for them two Tebeau boys."

"And that is about what I aim to be," McCanless said. "Only thing is, I don't want you telling about this here," and he tapped his shoulder. "Or your friend Harley Sorensen will be measuring me 'fore I am ready."

"I say you ought to resign."

McCanless just looked at him with his blue eyes, saying nothing.

"If I tell the council about your physical condition they will insist. They are not idiots and they ain't heartless either."

"Then who would be marshal? Who would be the law?"

McGee had no answer to that.

"It would be the end of Horsehead and the Herkimer County ranchers," McCanless said.

"I don't see it."

McCanless began building a smoke. "First of all, Doc, you are not going to tell anyone about this," and he nodded toward his shoulder. "But now"—he paused to take the string of the tobacco sack in his teeth and draw the sack closed then, finishing the cigarette, he went on—"don't you see, Tebeau is coming here no matter who is marshal. I can be lying in bed resting my shoulder and he'll still come here."

"So what if he does?"

"Study it a minute. Turn it over. Who told him I was here in Horsehead? O'Bannion or Galston or brother Gorm. Or all three. Am I right?"

"You are more than likely right; but so . . . ?"

"So the Eastern and Prairie will take over the whole of the small cattlemen—I mean, right now—using this trouble as the excuse for law and order. But it'll be their law and order."

Doc McGee cleared his nose, his throat, hacking, then spat redfaced into a spittoon. "Go on, go on," he said impatiently.

"It is what they will do. And if nobody stops them they will get away with it."

"But how?"

"It's easy. Tebeau comes. He is a top gunman. He is not like Gorm and the others. Make no mistake on that.

He is real quick. Galston and O'Bannion will use him.
The regulators will really regulate. It will be a army."

"None of us figured O'Bannion was the type to use
gunmen," McGee said, unable to disagree at all with what
he had just heard, but not knowing what to say.

"O'Bannion," McCanless said, "has got to be desperate.
Galston and the eastern money caught him in his fight
with the small outfits, and while they knocked themselves
out, Galston and his company took it all. That's how they
got O'Bannion, while he was busy fighting the small cattlemen." He canted his head at the doctor and his ash fell
from the cigarette in the corner of his mouth. "If they got
Tebeau in here, and they sure as hell will get him, then
they'll take the whole town. They'll move in as regulators,
peacemakers, vigilantes, whatever you want to name it.
And they'll take the whole damn county."

"Why don't you tell that to the council?"

"What will they do? Start a war? They want that like
they want poison."

Doc was silent a moment and then he said softly, "You
are going to get yourself killed."

"Maybe. Maybe not."

"But if I tell the council, maybe they'll see they have to
get you deputies."

"Name one. People may often act foolish, but they're
not all that suicidal. I have asked around."

"It's so damn complicated." Doc released a long sigh.
"Everyone against everyone else. Nobody knowing which
hand is doing which."

"That is exactly how men like Galston get their way,"
McCanless said.

He could see that his argument was finally striking
home. Doc was nodding.

"You think Cupid Tebeau is the only one gunning for
me, do you?"

"Well, there is Gorm."

"And there is Roderick Galston." McCanless paused. "They will take over the whole entire county. The council won't stop 'em. They can't."

Doc McGee sighed. "I know. I know it." And he let his eyes wander about the room as though in search of some kind of help. "What can I do?" he said after a moment. "I am no good with a gun. But I'll do what you say."

"I want you to talk to Skinner and Greenbow. Tell them what I told you. Get that picture to them."

"Wouldn't it be better if you . . ."

"We have got no time. You must tell them. They will listen to you."

"Take care of that shoulder then," Doc McGee said, not knowing what else he could say as McCanless started out of the office.

"It's that shoulder that's maybe going to take care of me," McCanless said.

The puzzled look was still on Doc's face as he walked out the door.

CHAPTER 21

He had been marshal of Horsehead for twenty-four hours and still he hadn't been inside his new office; but now, following his visit with McGee, he decided the time had come. The question in front of him was just where he would confront Cupid Tebeau, for it had to be his decision, not Tebeau's. And as he walked along the street in the midafternoon with the sunlight hot on his shoulders and arms, he kept turning this over, while at the same time feeling the curious eyes on him. The news, he realized, had traveled, and of course passersby were able to see the star he had pinned to his shirt.

The marshal's office was situated opposite the Thermopolis House, wedged between Sorensen's Funeral Establishment and Winkler's, a dry goods store which also dealt in secondhand clothing. In the former case, it was handy, McCanless noted, since a fair share of the marshal's business dealt with "former citizens now deceased"; and in the latter it was useful too, for upon occasion the late citizens' garments were all that was available to pay for the burial.

To his great surprise he discovered visitors waiting for him. As he pushed open the scarred, chipped wooden door of his office, he came face to face with Country O'Toole and the Great Grimaldi.

"What are you doing here?" he demanded coldly. "I thought you was out at the outfit taking care of the stock."

Grimaldi's long hands instantly rose in pacification. He bowed his bald head, his mustache twitched and his whole face spread in a friendly smile. "Ah, Marshal McCanless, sir. Everything is handled. Do not worry. All is handled at the ranch."

Meanwhile, O'Toole had whipped a big grin across his face in agreement.

"You think so?" McCanless was not in the mood for jollity. "You sitting here on them crates when your ass should be in a saddle ain't what you are s'posed to be doing."

"Sandy," explained Grimaldi. "She is taking care. She guards the ranch."

"The hell you say." McCanless pulled a chair—the only chair in the room—over to the desk by hooking his foot around one of its legs, and sat. The other two were seated on a pair of wooden packing boxes, that were evidently there for that purpose.

"It is all right," O'Toole said, cutting in on Grimaldi's flow. "She told us to come. She like ordered it. And we wanted to anyways."

McCanless' frown looked like thunder, and for a moment his two cowboys had to look at each other for reassurance.

"Just what the hell are you doing here is what I want to know!" He had taken out his .45 and was checking the load as he spoke to them, while they began to feel more and more uneasy.

"We have come to help you," the Great Grimaldi said, suddenly finding his courage to be able to speak at all, at first haltingly, and then adding, "Marshal McCanless," with bravura.

McCanless, leaning on his desk, put down the handgun and had a hard time holding back a smile.

"Glory be to God," he said, and was amazed at himself

resorting to a phrase he had seldom heard and had never used in his entire life. "The both of you?"

"That is correct," Country O'Toole said. "Maybe we ain't so good at guns and hosses and all of that, but we can help even so. Me, I can beat up on someone. I mean, that was a lucky punch Yankee Bill landed . . ."

"Boys, I appreciate it," McCanless said, overlapping O'Toole. "But where I need you is out at the ranch. Tebeau could hit us there, and the place needs to be watched. He could set a fire."

"But Miss Sandy said . . ." Grimaldi's hands raced through the air.

"And you'd be leaving a woman out there all by herself. Did you give that a thought?"

"We argued that with her and she said no, to come on in; she said she could handle it out there. And that makes sense," O'Toole said, "on account of this feller Tebeau is gonna be looking for you. And he will for sure know you are the marshal and not likely to be setting around at some ranch, but working right here in town. Right?" Country O'Toole was almost out of breath after he got through spilling that mouthful, and he looked at Grimaldi for confirmation.

The high-wire artiste nodded eagerly, his bald head shiny with sweat—it was hot in the little office—and flashed his very white teeth beneath his trim black mustache as he said, "It is true, Marshal McCanless. We are here to help. Tell us what to do. And then—consider it done!"

McCanless had picked up the handgun and was checking the action. By God, he was thinking. By God. Some people sure are a wonder.

"Some people sure are a wonder," he said aloud. "You know you'll both likely get ventilated. What you have been going through out at the ranch is nothing compared to what's coming up."

They turned their heads to look helplessly at one another. Then, as if by signal, both simultaneously shrugged. It was Grimaldi again who took the lead in speaking, his heavy Italian accent stumbling over the words, but getting them out all the same.

"Miss Sandy, sir. She it is who tell us to come. And when we question she get angry."

"We didn't want to leave her alone," O'Toole said, "but she insisted. She said she'd be . . ."

At which point the door of the office opened and the subject of conversation herself walked in.

"Don't tell me you've come to help too," McCanless said. And he dropped the .45 into the holster at his hip.

"That is what I am doing." And she stood there looking right at him, almost daring him to dispute her.

McCanless left it alone for a minute. Then he said, "I see a can of gunpowder coffee over there."

"I'll see what I can do."

They were silent for several moments while the coffee was boiling. McCanless rose and checked the gun cabinet, the drawers of the desk. The weaponry consisted of a .41 Colt sidearm, a Henry rifle, and two skinning knives, plus a few rounds of ammo for the guns. Then he checked the cell which was behind the office, in the yard. Built of wood, it was all the same a fairly solid structure.

"Like I said, I appreciate your offering," he told them, when he returned from his inspection. "But I need a free hand. I don't want to be worrying about the ranch; and I can't be riding herd on you two while trying to deal with Tebeau and Tebeau. Right?"

The two men nodded, but he saw that he had crushed them.

"I don't mean, you can't help me," he said quickly then. "The thing is—how."

They brightened a little at that. And he saw that he had even mollified Sandy.

"I need someone to watch the ranch. They will come to town since this is where I am making my play. But they might try something out there to draw me out. Like I said, maybe start a fire. You work with me in town here, Tebeau and the others—and there will be others with him —will just pick you off."

Sandy was nodding. "He is right," she said, looking at Grimaldi and O'Toole. Now she turned her eyes to McCanless. "Well, you see. You see, they—we—wanted you to know we were backing you. Whatever you need . . ." She stopped, looking down at her hands, which were lying in her lap. Then, lifting her head, she said firmly, "We will take care of the ranch. You mustn't worry about it."

"I am thinking you ought to move into town," he said. "They can stay out there."

"No." She said just the one word. Like that. And he said nothing to that. He knew there was nothing to say.

CHAPTER 22

There would be no letup now. And there was no way he could tell how much time he had. He knew it couldn't be much. The newspaper account of Tebeau's break couldn't have reached Horsehead all that much ahead of Cupid himself. So he could expect him any day now—any hour. He could even be here already.

As town marshal, he had to make his rounds, so after Sandy and his two cowhands had departed for the ranch he loaded extra ammo for the .45 into his pockets and started along Main Street.

It was evening now, the sky retreating into the advancing night as the sun withdrew across the rooftops of the town, over the prairie, rising to the tops of the rimrocks where that dawn it had descended; for a while leaving the heat behind, but this too would depart later when it got to be dark.

Making his rounds he came upon the friendly, the guarded, and the curious. A drunk in the Buffalo Bar had to be jailed; and at the Golden Wedding he broke up a fight between two Texans.

But where? The question ran through him like a pulsation. Where to make his stand? For he needed every advantage he could take. Cupid Tebeau would not be alone. At the same time, his help would likely be well hidden. Gorm, and probably others with him, would be ready to backshoot him from ambush if need be. Cupid Tebeau would take no chances. He never had in the old days.

It would be Tebeau himself in the center of the action. And Galston? Galston would be in the background pulling strings. Galston would be manipulating, maneuvering. What about O'Bannion? O'Bannion wanted shut of Galston; no question there. That man, McCanless was thinking, that man must be pretty damn desperate come now. Only where? Again and again, the burning question. Where?

There were so many elements, just like Doc McGee had said. Too damn many. Tebeau. His brother. Galston. O'Bannion. The ranchers and the council. And—Tebeau; always Tebeau. It was pretty sure Galston and Tebeau both had figured he, McCanless, was waiting for the confrontation in town. And they would play it that way. They would know too about his shoulder. They would know that he was alone.

But where in town? And how? And suddenly he asked himself what he was doing there in all that mess. Why didn't he just pack out of there? Get Gorm later. Keep it simple. Why did he have to get involved in a damn range fight? He could settle it with Gorm for Wiley and get on back to the Sweetwater. And to hell with Cupid Tebeau and O'Bannion and Galston.

Then all at once he remembered something he had said to Doc when they had met in his office the last time.

"It's so damn complicated," Doc had said. "Everybody siding against everybody else. Can't keep it straight. O'Bannion against the mavericks and the Eastern and Prairie against everyone else. And now Tebeau. How can a man figger what hand is doing which?"

And he had replied, "That is exactly how men like Galston come out on top. By playing everyone off."

Now, suddenly, he realized what he had said to McGee. Suddenly he remembered Wiley. Wiley's "learnin'." And with a dash of alarm, he realized he had been thinking the whole thing in a wrong way. Right now he was sitting game. A target big as the butte down at Elk Basin, and almost as stationary. It couldn't be worse, he told himself, almost saying the words out loud. Oh Christ, it couldn't be worse. And remembering Wiley then, he muttered, "And maybe by God it couldn't be better." And he knew what he was going to do.

There was still some light in the sky, but the town and the prairie stretching all around it were softening toward the coming night.

McCanless made his first stop at Doc McGee's office with a message for Sandy and the Circle Double O crew.

"I spoke with Greenbow and Skinner," McGee told him, shaking his head gloomily. "I guess it's like you were figuring. They don't want to be caught on the dirty end of the stick. Like they see it, it's one thing to hold down law and order, but it's a different horse when it gets to open warfare. They got families."

"And you?"

Doc got sore at that. "Like I told you already, Goddammit."

"Then you'll deliver that message?"

McGee nodded.

Leaving, he ran into Harley Sorensen.

"I hear tell that feller Tebeau is hereabouts."

"So."

"Sent a message to you, but you weren't in your office, so it come to me, being next door." Sorensen's lugubrious look lengthened while he stood there on the boardwalk in his black coat and trousers, with one eye slightly closed as he looked at McCanless.

"So what's the message?"

"Said he was riding into town tomorrow in the A.M. and he'll be looking for you."

McCanless felt good then. He knew he had made the right decision. He saw Sorensen watching his shoulder.

"How's that arm?" the undertaker asked.

"What made you think there was anything wrong with it?"

"You moving it kind of stiff-like."

"It is fine," McCanless said. Nodding, he turned and walked toward the Thermopolis House. Let them all figure he was crippled; he needed every help.

The fact that it was the gloomy undertaker who brought him the news of Tebeau was not lost on him. He almost smiled, thinking how much Wiley would have enjoyed that touch.

CHAPTER 23

Dawn broke red across the land, inhabiting the sky with the majesty of the new day. In Horsehead a dog barked, a cock crowed again from behind the livery barn, as the fresh morning slipped into the awakening town. And for McCanless there was a moment when the morning sounds and smells met the growing light in a unique resonance, penetrating him and bringing something unnamed from long ago. As he rode the little dun out of the town, along the narrow trail leading west, toward the Broken Spade.

He had made his plan and at the same time he had discarded it. He was therefore free to respond cleanly to whatever happened. Alone. With no longings, no regrets. He carried nothing with him that was not needed. He had his horse, his weapons; and he had his purpose. He had himself and nothing more was necessary. He knew well that there would always be time enough for dying. He was free; free to face O'Bannion, Galston, Gorm, and Cupid Tebeau. McCanless knew this: that like everyone else he would one day die—maybe this day—and the only question that mattered was how.

No riders. To the good that was. He did not really expect any. Although they might still be out at the Spade, they would figure him being in town waiting for Tebeau. Wiley'd always put it that surprise was the greatest help a man could have, provided he knew how to use it.

He saw no one until he rode into the Broken Spade

proper and a man with white hair and a cane came out of the bunkhouse to stand watching him. Probably a horse wrangler or cook, injured and so left back by the crew, who probably were out gathering stock or maybe up at Tensleep line-camp. McCanless saw the man's surprise in the way he stood, moving his white head a little as though looking for somebody to tell it to.

He rode up to the house and sat his horse for a minute or two, waiting to see whether anyone else was about. The old man at the bunkhouse was still watching him.

He was about to dismount when suddenly the door of the house opened and Cole O'Bannion stood there.

"What do you want, McCanless?"

"I have come to arrest Gorm Tebeau on suspicion of murder."

Cole O'Bannion took a step forward, as always not armed. "He is not here. The men are not here."

"I have got a warrant and if you don't turn him over I will take him. I know he is either here or on his way to Horsehead."

"Where did you get that warrant, McCanless?" O'Bannion, looking haggard and carrying his seventy years a bit heavy that day, moved out of the doorway.

"I made it out—as town marshal."

"Maybe you are the marshal, but you are not the law."

In one swift movement McCanless stepped down from the dun pony. "I am the law within my jurisdiction," he said, cold. "And that includes the Broken Spade."

Cole O'Bannion spread his big hands. "Search then. If you find him, let me know." And he stood there working his big jaws.

At that moment a shot rang out from behind the house. It was immediately followed by another; and another.

McCanless looked at O'Bannion.

"Target practice," the rancher said. "Roderick is prac-
ticing. What he does every day."

Cutting his eye to the bunkhouse, McCanless saw that
the old man with the cane had gone. "We will go there
then," he said.

He was carrying the scatter-gun in his left hand with
his forefinger on the trigger, leaving his right free for the
.45. This was all his armament, but it was enough; and he
would not be hampered by extra weight.

More pistol shots rang out as they reached the back of
the house. O'Bannion stopped then and turned to face
McCanless. "Gorm is not here," he said again.

McCanless knew the rancher was stalling. He motioned
with the scatter-gun toward the stand of box elders about
two hundred yards behind the house. "We'll have a look-
see at the target range," he said as two more shots rang
out from beyond the trees.

Moving into the trees now, McCanless saw they were
at the edge of a shallow draw with more box elders on the
far side. In the clearing Galston had set up his targets.
There were a few of the standard bullseyes on posts
which had been set into the ground, and a variety of bottles along the top of a board fence. Other bottles were
lined up on a fallen log; and still others hung from string
tied to the branches of a single tree almost in the center
of the clearing. Two posts had playing cards attached to
them and Stetson hats on top with bullet holes in them.

Roderick Galston, wearing a white shirt with rolled-up
sleeves, was standing at a table on which were a number
of assorted handguns and a good amount of ammunition.
He was in the act of reloading.

McCanless was watching O'Bannion closely. The
rancher had begun to fidget a little and he wanted to
make sure there would be no signaling Galston. At the
same time he was keeping an eye on their back trail. For,

what had happened to the old man with the cane? Gone to get the Tebeaus? Or others? Maybe Tebeau and Gorm had ridden into town? They could easily have taken a different trail and he would not have seen them.

And now at that very moment of his thought a figure appeared in the clearing, stepping through the trees at the opposite side. He was wearing a crisp black Stetson hat and a black shirt and pants. He was followed by Gorm, still wearing the gray derby with the bullet holes, still chewing relentlessly, with his trousers sagging, his knobby elbows piercing his aged shirt.

"Got them hosses ready," Gorm said. "Couldn't find that old man. Probably off drinking somewheres."

McCanless watched the back of O'Bannion's neck tighten, and he said, "No." The rancher's neck reddened.

Then Galston said, "Ah, Tebeau. I was hoping you would come to give me a few pointers."

The man in black did not answer. He was peering at the trees that fringed the clearing, his lean body straight, stiff as a riding whip.

"What's wrong?" Galston said, suddenly looking at him.

Cupid Tebeau shook his head. "Just had a feeling," he said. "I will be riding into town directly. We'll save the target practice for when I get back."

"I shall be waiting," Galston said pleasantly. Raising the pistol he had just loaded, he sighted carefully at a post which had two playing cards attached to it. "I will be waiting with the expectation of excellent news, Tebeau." And he squeezed the trigger; once, twice.

McCanless, watching from where he and O'Bannion were hidden in the trees, didn't have to be told they were bullseyes. It was all in the way the Britisher lowered the weapon while giving a smug little nod of his head.

McCanless' voice broke suddenly into the clearing as he

prodded O'Bannion with the scatter-gun and stepped out of the trees.

"It has been a while, Algernon."

Cupid Tebeau had started for his holster, but his hand froze as McCanless appeared in full view from behind O'Bannion.

"I have got you all bunched in my sights," he said. "Thanks to Mister Galston there and his—uh—hobby." And he watched the color hit the Englishman's face. "This scatter will cut you right off if there is one single move." There was a wicked smile on his face.

Cupid Tebeau's face was dark with fury and Gorm's fingers drummed along the sides of his legs. It was Roderick Galston who remained at ease.

A smile moved swiftly onto his face as he said, "McCanless. You did finally decide to come for some shooting with me. How good of you." He let a little laugh fall into the tableau. "You know, this is actually my first confrontation with a real gunman. I mean, in action. Now you, Tebeau, and your brother there, you are professionals. What would you do in such a situation?"

Swifter than light Tebeau pulled Galston in front of him and had his six-gun pointing at McCanless. Meanwhile O'Bannion had plunged out of the line of fire.

"You sonofabitch," Cupid Tebeau said. "Drop that scatter."

But McCanless did not move. "I don't mind cutting the both of you right off at the neck." He spat suddenly at random. "I am taking Gorm into town." From the side of his eye he saw Gorm's hands move slightly. "Not a move, Gorm. Not a move except to unbuckle or you'll see that brother of yours ventilated like a sieve."

"You sonofabitch," snarled Cupid Tebeau. "Put down that damn thing and draw like a man!"

"He is ascairt to," Gorm said. But he was unbuckling his gun belt as he spoke the words.

Now McCanless said, "Tebeau, drop that gun. You have got three seconds." And he raised the scatter ever so slightly.

By God, he was thinking. Maybe he won't. But he knew Tebeau. He had played cards with him. And he knew Tebeau always wanted to win; had to win. He wouldn't risk it. No, not now. And sure enough, Cupid Tebeau's six-gun dropped into the grass.

"Oh come now, McCanless," Galston said, with a laugh in his voice, albeit a nervous laugh. "You're spoiling all the fun. Here, I've never witnessed a real western gun-fight, and now this is the moment I've been so looking forward to. I want to see you and Tebeau have it out. Look," and he almost took a step forward. "I'll pay you. I will pay both of you gentlemen money to have your gunfight right here, right now. What do you say!"

Too late McCanless heard the step in back of him. The blow on his left shoulder knocked the scatter-gun to the ground, and before he could recover he heard Harry Dime say, "Good thing I had me a hoss-size hangover this A.M. and didn't ride out with the men."

McCanless watched Cupid Tebeau move toward his gun, which was lying on the grass.

Harry Dime's voice came from behind. "Just drop it into your holster, Tebeau. And McCanless, remember I got this .45 right on you."

Only Harry Dime couldn't leave it alone. "Told you I'd even it one day, McCanless," he said. And now he stepped around so that McCanless could see him.

"Bully for you."

Out of the side of his eye, he saw Gorm edging toward his right.

"Harry, let Tebeau handle it," O'Bannion said.

And so, the cards lay there. He and Cupid Tebeau, with Gorm already behind him now to backshoot if necessary. Pretty neat it was. By God. But he wasted no time cussing. He was, in fact, remembering something Wiley had taught him a long time ago. It had been invented and perfected by an old gunfighter named Billy Roller and it was known in just a few circles as the Roller roll. It was a tough one, which was why it wasn't too well known; but then as Wiley'd never tired of saying, "It don't hurt to know everything." Well, let them go on thinking he had his busted-up shoulder. Yet, there was Harry Dime. If only the foreman would stay out of it.

"Well now, sonny . . ." Cupid Tebeau had taken a couple of steps forward and was facing him directly. "Seems like now it is my turn, too," he said, "to even it. Except I am going to do better than even it." His mouth cut into a grin and a hard laugh fell from him. "How's that shoulder I hear you got lead in?"

"It is good enough," McCanless said, and he added, "Algernon."

In that same second that Cupid Tebeau struck at his holstered six-gun, McCanless, looser than he had ever been in his life, stroked the .45 out and up and shot him right through the heart. And within the very same second McCanless dropped, twisting his body as he fell on his back, but still raised enough to put a bullet through Gorm, whose own shot—fired in ultimate surprise—soared into nowhere.

He had landed on his shoulder and now rolled over to get to his feet again, his eyes searching for Harry Dime. Only it was not the Broken Spade foreman who provided the following action. As McCanless finished off both Tebeaus, it was Roderick Galston who drew his silver-handled six-gun—his favorite—from its soft, tooled leather holster, shouting, "McCanless!"

The shot that next rang into the little clearing came from neither Galston nor McCanless, but from Cole O'Bannion. Without a second's hesitation the rancher had stepped to the table, picked up a loaded Smith & Wesson and shot Roderick Galston right through his forehead.

When McCanless got to his feet, the rancher tossed the gun back onto the table with its companions.

A long silence followed as McCanless, O'Bannion, and Harry Dime surveyed the carnage.

When, in a few moments, Country O'Toole and the Great Grimaldi arrived on the scene, O'Bannion said, "I will go in with you now, if you want, McCanless."

McCanless didn't wait much on that. "I don't reckon I will be needing you anymore as deputy, O'Bannion." And he turned to O'Toole and Grimaldi. "Wasn't sure you got my message to follow."

"Doc told us. We caught up some old man out there. Hope it was soon enough."

McCanless didn't say anything. He looked at Harry Dime. "Reckon we are square now, Harry. Let's keep it that way." He looked at the three bodies. "There has been enough of this here."

Cole O'Bannion said, "You run your spread, McCanless, and I'll run the Broken Spade; depending on the Eastern and Prairie," he added. "But it is going to be different, by God. It is gonna be different." His eyes swept the clearing. "Harry, first thing you get some men clear all this out of here. I mean, now!"

Cole O'Bannion reached into his shirt pocket and took out a cigar. He bit off the end and lighted it. Harry Dime was watching him. There was another cigar in the rancher's pocket, but he didn't offer it to his foreman.

Harry Dime liked that. He had gotten one cigar from Cole O'Bannion in fifteen years. Good enough. He didn't like weakness in a man, especially a cattleman.

A while later, when McCanless and his two cowboys rode into the Circle Double O, he found Sandy Taggart waiting for them. He let Country O'Toole and the Great Grimaldi tell what had happened, getting most of it wrong, but he didn't correct them. It was over and he was shut of it.

"Can we ask you somethin'?" O'Toole said.

McCanless waited.

Country O'Toole cut his eye to his companion and said, "What's going to happen here? Are you going to stay? We was wondering about us?"

McCanless studied it a moment and then he said, "Thought you two might hang around a spell. I'll be moseyin' back to the Sweetwater to have a look-see."

Grimaldi and O'Toole exchanged looks again, while McCanless had his eyes on the silent girl.

"We had hopes you settle here," the Great Grimaldi said. "With us. We are your cowboys."

"A man ought to settle down," O'Toole muttered.

Then McCanless said something he suddenly realized he had known for a long time. "Man's been around everywhere, he's at home anywhere." He stood up, and reaching into his shirt pocket took out his makings and began building a smoke.

The two men and the girl continued to sit at the table with their coffee, not saying anything.

At last Sandy said, without looking up, "When are you leaving?"

"Now," he said, striking the lucifer on the seat of his denim pants. "I only got one problem."

Now she looked at him, caught by something in his voice. "What is your problem?"

"You."

Her eyes were glistening and he didn't know whether she was going to cry or laugh.

"I don't figure I am a problem," she said.

He said, "I'll be riding the dun. Reckon the roan might be a good one for you."

"That is what I reckon, too," she said, imitating him.

When they all laughed, he felt different. Then he said, "While you're gettin' your gear together I will saddle the horses." And he started out the door.

His two cowboys had risen to follow, but now McCanless stopped in the doorway. He took off his Stetson hat and settled it back on his head.

She heard the difference in his voice when he said, "Want you to see the Sweetwater country. There ain't no place like it anywheres."

About the Author

James Wyckoff is the author of numerous short stories and has written for radio and TV as well. His most recent Double D Western was SHARKEY. Mr. Wyckoff lives in New York City.